SHAMROCKS ARE A GIRL'S BEST FRIEND

LUCINDA RACE

MC TWO PRESS

Editor Susan of West of Mars
Proofreader Kimberly Dawn

Cover design by Jade Webb www.meetcutecreative.com

Manufactured in the United States of America
First Edition June 2022

Print Edition ISBN 978-1-954520-13-4

E-book ISBN 978-1-954520-12-7

AUTHOR'S NOTE

Hi and welcome to my world of romance with a touch of magic. I hope you love my characters as much I love them. So, turn the page and fall in love again.

If you'd like to stay in touch, please join my Newsletter. I release it twice per month with tidbits, recipes and an occasional special gift just for my readers so sign up here: https://lucindarace.com/newsletter/ and there's a free book when you join!

Happy reading...

---

elly O'Malley crept down the hallway of Shamrock Cottage, her heart pounding in her chest. The early morning sun streamed through the skylights and the hardwood floor was cool against her bare feet on this late-January morning. The weight of her cell phone was comforting in her sweatpants pocket.

Who the heck was in her house?

She slid along the wall like she had seen in those movies on television where the girl sleuth was stalking the unknown. *Dramatic much?* When she reached the end of the hall, she peeked around the corner, her gaze sweeping the open space of the living and dining rooms and kitchen. Standing in front of the sliding glass doors, looking out over the ocean, was a very tall man, even by her standards, as Kelly was tapping six feet herself. With a backpack over one shoulder and an enormous canvas duffel bag at his feet, he leaned heavily on a cane.

She tiptoed to the counter and grabbed the cast iron skillet, being careful not to make a sound. If he'd heard her, he hadn't moved.

She raised the skillet to shoulder height, clutching it with two hands for good swinging leverage. "What are you doing in my house?"

The man slowly turned, grimaced, clutched his leg, and held up his other hand with the cane dangling from it. "What are you doing in my rental?" Confusion and pain clouded his eyes. "I promise I can't hurt you." He gestured to his leg. "Recovering from surgery and exhausted from a long drive."

She didn't lower her makeshift weapon but instead looked him over from head to toe. He was ruggedly handsome but did look road weary. "Rental?"

"Yes, well, actually this place belongs to a friend of my uncle, who's a fire chief in Chicago. I signed the agreement on Rental Direct." He shifted his backpack on his shoulder. "I can show you the agreement on my laptop."

Well, that was the company her aunt and uncle used to rent their cottage, but that was before her house had burned to the ground in November and left her homeless.

"Who's your uncle?"

He'd better come up with the right names or she'd call the police to escort him out and then change the code for the door lock. That thought caused her to frown; she'd changed it at the beginning of December.

"John Bannon, and he's friends with Kevin O'Malley and his wife. I can't remember her name."

Well, that was her uncle. She kept holding the skillet with one hand and with the other withdrew her cell. "Joan. Her name is Joan. I'm going to give him a call and I'll put it on speakerphone."

"Good idea." He took a slow, halting step toward her and a flash of agony washed over his face.

She softened but still brandished the skillet even

though her arm was beginning to tremble. She lowered it. "No funny business."

He held up his hands in surrender. "Promise." He gestured to a chair. "Mind if I sit?"

She pointed to a stool on the other side of the breakfast bar. Kelly didn't want to look like she was a pushover, but his face was stark white and the last thing she wanted was for him to collapse.

Placing the cell on the counter, she stared at the man across from her. After the fourth ring, a deep male voice said, "Kelly, this is a surprise."

"Hi, Uncle Kevin. I've got a situation down here."

"There's a list of qualified repair people on the island. You don't need to call us before you take care of business."

"It's not that kind of issue. I have a man in my cottage and he says you rented this place to him." Then it dawned on her that he hadn't said his name. "Who are you?"

"Patrick Ryan, but my friends call me Tric." He gave her a strained smile.

"Did you hear that? Patrick Ryan is in my home."

"Oh, shoot, Kel. I'm sorry. Up until this moment, I'd forgotten we'd given Tric the family and friends code before your fire, which let him book even though I had put a hold on new rentals. He needed a place to recover once he was well enough to travel, and you know the magic of Last Chance Beach has a way of healing all wounds."

"You forgot to tell me you rented the house to a stranger. What are we supposed to do?" Inwardly, she sighed. There was no way her uncle would ever rent the house to anyone sketchy.

"Any chance you two can stay under the same roof for a few days? I'll make a few calls and see if I can find a new rental for Patrick."

She rolled her shoulders. Not that her uncle could see it but it made her feel better. "I guess, but do me a favor and make sure the rental listing is hidden on RD. I don't want anyone else showing up as a surprise houseguest."

He gave a hearty chuckle. "I promise that won't happen and I'm sure in no time, you two will adjust to living under one roof, at least for a few days."

Under her breath, she muttered, "Don't count on it." Louder, she said, "Give Aunt Joan a hug for me."

"Will do, and we'll talk soon."

She hit the end button and studied Patrick Ryan. He was easy on the eyes, with his dark-brown hair in an old-fashioned style, deep-blue eyes with crinkles at the corners, and a crooked nose that had obviously been broken at one time. Why did he have to sport deep dimples in both cheeks? It was her weakness in any guy—the deeper the dimple, the harder she'd fall.

"So, Patrick, it seems that we're stuck together for a while until my uncle can make some calls to other cottage owners."

"Please call me Tric. And I take it you're Kelly."

She nodded. "Kelly O'Malley and yes"—she held up her thumb and index finger with a small space between them—"I'm a wee bit Irish." She found herself smiling. "What kind of nickname is that? Why not Rick or Pat?"

He shrugged his shoulders. "I'm kind of a jokester around my crew and it sort of stuck."

"Police or fire?"

"Fireman for the last twenty years. Well, until I got hurt."

She leaned against the counter. "What happened?"

"Stupid accident. I broke my femur, ribs, and punctured a lung for good measure. A bunch of hardware later and I'm here to tell the tale."

He was nonchalant about his injury. But she could see the truth in his eyes; it had been bad and recovery was taking a long time.

"Well, how about since we're stuck together, I'll give you the grand tour. There's plenty of room for both of us." She gave him a polite smile. They might be forced roommates, but they didn't need to be super cozy with each other.

"If possible, could you tell me which cupboard the glasses are in first? I need to take a pain pill after being in the car so long."

"Oh, jeez. I'll get it for you." She opened a cabinet above the sink and pulled out a glass, which she filled from the jug of water in the refrigerator. "Don't drink water from the tap; it's always tepid, but if you see the jug getting low, fill it up. I've got a backup jug too."

"I'll just pick up some bottled water." He accepted the glass and popped a pill in his mouth and took a long drink. "Thanks."

"Don't waste money on buying water. There are reusable bottles in the cabinet." She put the jug back into the fridge and crossed the spacious room to the glass doors. "Out that way is the beach and ocean, in case you missed it." She cocked her head. "Where did you say you're from?"

"I didn't, but a suburb of Chicago."

"As you can tell, we've got no snow or frigid temperatures. Just mild winds and lots of sun every day. It's like being on vacation." She grinned. "Well, you are on vacation."

She pointed to the television. "We have satellite and I'll give you the password for the WiFi." She walked in the direction of the other side of the house and stopped before going down the hall. "There are four bedrooms, a couple of bathrooms, and in the main bath, there is a washer and dryer. I have the bedroom on the left and I've also taken over the smaller room next to that for my office, but you can choose either of the other rooms. Both have a decent view." She pointed to the rooms that were on the right. "Take your pick."

"Your office? What do you do for work?" He hobbled to where she stood.

With each step he took, she held her breath, waiting for him to topple over. "Freelance website designer for all types of small businesses, authors, audiobook narrators, and I also do a little cover design. My background is in graphic art. I'm pretty quiet when I work so I shouldn't disturb you."

"I'm more concerned I might bother you, so I'll be invisible during working hours."

She waved a hand at him. "That's really nice but I usually listen to music while I work, so I never hear a thing, and I'll use headphones if you're still sleeping."

He eased open the door to the bedroom farthest from the heart of the home. "I'll take this one." He slowly walked back down the hall. "I need my bags."

Kelly held out a hand. "I'll get them for you." She hurried to where he had dropped them and came back half dragging the duffel. "What do you have in here, a dead body or something?"

"A few books and clothes."

She gave him a long look and crossed her arms over her chest. "How long were you planning on staying in Last Chance Beach?"

"At least two months. I have to finish healing and then get strong enough to pass a physical and endurance test to get back to active duty in the department. If I can't, I may be washed up."

She placed his bags just inside the bedroom. With a reassuring smile, she said, "If there's any place that will work its magic, it's here. I swear there's something in the air that just makes all problems evaporate, or maybe it's the ocean and our troubles just get washed away."

"I hope you're right." He waited until she was back in the hall before he entered the room. "I'm going to unpack, but I'll catch up with you later."

"If you need something, I'll be in my office. With the door open." Why she felt the need to add that was beyond her. But something about him tugged at her heart.

"Thanks, Kelly. I'm sorry about earlier. I had no idea there was anyone here when I came inside. I feel bad I scared you."

"What, you thought I was scared because I was wielding a skillet? That's always how I greet people. It makes me memorable."

He gave her a weak smile. "It's one greeting I won't forget anytime soon." He closed the door and then opened it. "Kelly, when do computers overheat?"

She tipped her head to one side. Was he worried about a fire in her home office? "Um?"

"When they need to vent." His smile grew a little wider, but it still didn't reach his eyes. He closed the door for a second time.

She stood there, staring at the white-painted door. She had noticed he looked like a man lost and not from his physical injury, but maybe there was more to what had happened than he said. Not that being a firefighter wasn't a dangerous job, but the haunted look on his face gave her the impression something else weighed heavy on his mind. She smiled when she thought of his joke. He had a lame sense of humor, but it was charming at the same time. But she had meant what she said—being at the beach restored souls and healed hearts. After all, wasn't that why she found herself living here?

Before going into her office to start the workday, she detoured to the kitchen. After the adrenaline rush from the early morning, she needed coffee, lots of dark roasted cups of caffeine. She paused midstep and was going to ask Tric if he wanted any but before she tapped on his door, she could already hear the gentle sound of snoring. The poor man was exhausted from driving straight through from Chicago and was weak as a kitten. She eased away and headed toward the coffee pot. Today, she'd work without music just until she got used to her temporary houseguest.

*T*ric dropped to the bed. Exhaustion washed over him as he hoped to get a surge of energy. Driving to Last Chance Beach from Chicago had been a dumb idea. Each mile on the odometer had drained him even though he'd thought he'd been up to the trip. The real reason he had driven was because he didn't know if he was going back to Chicago. Pretty much all his important belongings were either in the trunk of his car or in his duffel bag. And as far as a much-needed change of scenery, being in the company of the tall, dark-haired beauty with soulful gray eyes was a good distraction. He fell back on the bed without taking off his shoes and closed his eyes, but his last thought was of Kelly's captivating smile.

---

2

*T*he next morning, Kelly was in the kitchen drinking coffee when she heard the soft tap, tap, tap of Tric's cane as he made his way down the hall at a turtle's pace. She had brewed a large pot of coffee, hoping he'd be up before she started work. He had never come out of his room after he went in yesterday morning. She had nailed it—he was exhausted. Last night, she had stood outside his door but she hadn't knocked; the sound of him snoring reassured her he was okay.

"Good morning, Patrick."

He lifted his hand in greeting. "Tric, please, and good morning." His gaze was laser-focused on the coffee pot. "May I?"

She poured him a mug and winked. "I hope you like it strong."

His eyes twinkled. "Is there any other way?" He took a tentative sip. "It's good."

"How did you sleep?"

He moved around the island and sat down with a small grimace. "Like a rock."

He was a man of few words and Kelly wondered if that was because it was early or that was just his way. While he concentrated on his coffee, she said, "I was thinking about our situation."

He lifted his gaze to meet her look. "I'll check with my uncle and try to find a new place today."

She noticed his voice was flat, almost defeated, which cemented her decision. "You rented the cottage in good faith and I know my uncle wouldn't have given you the family code if you weren't a good guy, so if you want to stay, that's fine with me. The cottage is big enough for both of us."

He tipped his head. "Really? You'd share your home with a stranger?"

"It's not forever and I think as two mature adults we can handle it."

He gave her a small smile. "Thanks. That would be great."

"And I'm happy to share my food until you get to the grocery store. I'm not sure I have what you like, but help yourself."

He rewarded her kindness with another warm smile, causing her heart to flutter.

"I'm a pretty healthy eater but I'll get out today. If you need something, I'm happy to pick it up for you."

"I appreciate that. Time to get ready for work." She tapped a paper on the counter. "This is my cell phone number if you need anything."

He glanced at it and this time gave her a wide grin. "Is that your way of saying don't bother you while you're in the office?"

"Not at all, and I don't have any conference calls scheduled today." She refilled her mug. "Make yourself at

SHAMROCKS ARE A GIRL'S BEST FRIEND

home."

"Thanks, Kelly. I really appreciate your generosity."

She clinked her mug to his. Tric might be just the distraction she needed to jump-start life again. "It's Irish hospitality."

*T*ric waited until Kelly was in her office before he exhaled a ragged breath. His leg was screaming in agony and he was stiff after the drive so he desperately needed to take a pain pill. He had to wonder about Kelly and her trusting nature—not that he wasn't grateful—but still, what kind of sane woman would let a man she didn't know stay with her? Unless she was really just a nice person who could tell she wasn't in any danger from him since his only priority was recovery.

He hobbled to the cabinet where the glasses were stored. He filled it with tap water and swallowed a pain pill. She was right. It was tepid.

His stomach grumbled and although he needed relief from the throbbing in his leg, he opened the refrigerator, withdrawing a carton of eggs, some veggies, and cheese.

"Kelly?" he called over his shoulder. "Would you like an omelet?"

No answer.

He made his way down the hall and tapped on the half-open door and eased it open the rest of the way. She had headphones on and her back was to the door. He didn't want to scare her so he said in a loud voice, "Kelly."

She dipped her shoulders, slipped the headphones down around her neck, and turned away from her computer. "What's up?"

"I'm fixing breakfast. Would you like an omelet?"

"I could eat something. I've got some cheese and tomatoes in the fridge."

She started to get up, but he held out his hand to stop her. "I'll cook and let you know when it's ready. Give me about fifteen minutes."

"Okay. I'll finish up what I'm working on and be out soon." She gave him a crooked smile. "Thanks."

He ambled back to the kitchen. *It's the least I can do since she's giving me time to get my bearings.* He chopped and sautéed onions and peppers and whisked five eggs together until they were light and frothy. As he pushed the bread down in the toaster, his stomach grumbled again, reminding him that the last time he had eaten was long before he had arrived at the cottage. He added the butter and as it sizzled, the egg mixture was next.

"That smells great." Kelly appeared at his elbow.

A zip of electricity raced up his arm at her nearness. He put distance between them and used the toast popping up as the excuse in his head. It was an unusual thing, to be this close to a woman he barely knew and have such a strong physical reaction.

Kelly added the shredded cheese to the eggs before folding them in half. "Can you hand me the plates?"

It was nice that they were working together; it was something he hadn't had in a long time and he realized it was nice to have someone share a simple meal with him.

*B*efore long, their plates were scraped clean and all that was left were toast crumbs. Kelly got up to pour more coffee. She offered him a refill, but he shook his head no. He really should drink more water.

She stirred in a splash of cream. "You can make breakfast for me anytime. That's the best omelet I've had in forever. Where did you learn to cook like that?"

"Hanging around my uncle's firehouse. Firemen are some of the best cooks you'll ever meet outside of a professional kitchen."

"I've heard rumors but didn't think it was true." She leaned back in the chair and sipped her coffee, then tilted her head as she studied his face. "How are you feeling? Your color's better than earlier."

"I'm okay. My pain pill kicked in. Almost ready to take on the world." He was surprised she noticed and it gave him a warm feeling in the pit of his stomach. "I'll clean up the kitchen and then take off for a while."

"You really should enjoy the deck. The breeze off the ocean is magic."

He chuckled. "A magical breeze. I had no idea."

Her eyes twinkled and she put a finger across her lips. "It's not just the breeze that's magic; locals believe there is magic on the island—to heal hearts, bodies, and even reunite lost loves. It's a little-known secret about this part of the country, and if it got out, more people would flock here all year round. Think of it like Ponce de Leon's Fountain of Youth."

He pretended to close a zipper over his lips. "Your secret is safe with me."

Her chair scraped over the floor as she pushed back and stacked the plates. "You can leave the door unlocked when you go out."

"I have the security code."

She frowned. "That's right. How could I forget?" She put the dishes in the sink and ran water over them. "Since you cooked, I'll clean up." She handed him a large blue vinyl-covered binder he had noticed on the counter. "My aunt put this together for guests. There are some maps in here to help you navigate the island."

As he took it, his hand grazed hers. She must have felt the zing too, as color flushed her cheeks.

"Thanks." He grinned and was pleased the reactions to a casual touch were mutual. "We seem to say that a lot."

She wiped her hand over where they had touched as if to quiet the unexpected but pleasant sensations—or was that his imagination? "I think it's part of getting to know someone so the other doesn't think you're taking a nice gesture for granted."

"True. Well, how about if we say cheers instead? That way, it'll break up the conversation."

She laughed. "A wise guy. I like it."

With a wide grin, he said, "Cheers."

She picked up her coffee mug. "Dishes and then back to work for me. See you later."

"Cheers."

His laughter followed her down the hall and he was still chuckling softly as she closed her office door. The good thing was he had a sense of humor. The bad news was that when he smiled, she got a funny feeling in the pit of her stomach, and there was no time for a dalliance with the handsome Tric Ryan, or was there? That dark-brown hair with sprinkles of silver at the temples and those deep-blue eyes were enough to cause any woman who drew breath to have a nice knee-knocking swoon. Her email pinged with an incoming message; it was from one of her biggest clients. Time to refocus on the task at hand.

The rest of the morning vanished and when Kelly

looked up from her computer, she noticed it was past one. The house was like a church, and the sound drifting through the window was of waves breaking against the shore. It must be high tide. She stretched her arms overhead and wondered why she hadn't heard Tric come back. Padding to the living room, the doors to the deck were open. He was in a lounge chair, sunglasses over his eyes. Her breath caught. He was the most handsome man she had ever seen, but it wasn't just his physical attributes. There was a solidness that was very attractive too.

"Are you coming out?"

His deep voice broke the silence, and she was caught ogling him. Damn. She thought he was snoozing.

She detoured to the kitchen to get a glass of tea. She poured two and noticed the fridge was packed full of food. He wasn't kidding when he said he ate healthy. Kelly strolled out to the deck with the tea.

"When did you get back?" She handed a glass to him and sat on the companion lounge chair.

"About an hour ago. The island is beautiful. I found the market and to return your gracious offer, help yourself to anything you want."

She looked out across the beach and thought of helping herself to his oh-so-kissable lips but quickly refocused. "How's the leg feeling?" She noticed he wasn't using his cane.

"Not bad."

If he wanted to keep things casual between them, these short conversations were the way to do it.

"How long have you lived on Last Chance Beach?"

She liked the simple Q and A. "For about ten years. I came down to heal a broken heart and my company shut down while I was on vacation, so I needed to change careers. That's when I started my own company, and now I work for who I want and life is simple."

"And your heart? Did LCB work its magic?" His voice was quiet as he looked across the beach.

"It did. I love the simplicity of island living, so I stayed. Life was going great until my house burned to the ground. They investigated and it was ruled accidental, a problem with faulty wiring. I had only been a homeowner for less than two years." She wasn't sure why she divulged all the details except this was the first time she'd spoken of it to anyone other than family and close friends.

He quirked a brow. "What did they say specifically about the electric?"

"It might have been the freezer. A couple days before the fire, I was smelling hot tuna in the garage. I guess it was wires starting to burn. I'm now in the process of rebuilding." She sighed with longing. "The view at my place isn't as nice as this one."

"Where is your home?"

"Inland, over near Second Street, and the farthest point from the fire department as possible. If they had gotten to my place sooner, it might not have been a total loss. I had to replace my work computers but thank goodness I use cloud storage, so my business wasn't interrupted."

"I guess that's a silver lining."

It felt good to talk about the fire, and he didn't seem to be judging her. She looked his way. "I was going to take a run over before dinner. Would you like to go?" She didn't want to confess it was hard to see the scorched ground of what used to be her house, but she felt better just knowing she'd put eyes on it at least once a week.

"Sure. Just give me a few minutes warning and I'll be ready."

"We can leave at four. Sunset is about six. If you want to witness your first one, I have just the spot. And either before or after, we can do a grand tour of the island?"

"That would make me feel like I was on vacation." He gave her a wink. "Cheers."

She couldn't help but grin. She was starting to look forward to their little adventure.

3

After a while, Kelly went back to her office. Tric waited until he heard the door close before heaving himself up from the lounge chair. He wanted to look up her fire. Something sounded odd. What had been the cause? On an island this size, the fire department should be able to reach any structure pretty quickly before it was a total loss, shouldn't they? He'd spent enough time with firefighters to know the smell of smoke did mean fire, or was he just looking for an excuse to be the hero? And what did it matter? It wasn't like he'd see her after he went back to work, if he went back to work.

He got his laptop and settled back in the lounge chair. The leg was feeling so much looser since he arrived at the beach. Stretching out, he scanned the newsfeed for the little town but quickly discovered the local paper wasn't daily and although Kelly's house fire was news, it was more about her being displaced and less about the cause. He then switched over to the mainland paper but came up empty. When they got to the house site, he was going to look very carefully at what was left of her home, or were his instincts battle-worn like his body? His eyes grew heavy and he let the sound of the waves wash over him.

Flying into a wildfire was nothing new. He wasn't a rookie in the back of a plane, geared up and ready to jump.

His partner Pete gave him the high sign and he leaped out into the blue sky on the edge of smoke. Without hesitation, Tric followed him, free-falling toward the landing site. The ground rushed up underneath him and his chute snapped open. Adrenaline pumped through his veins. But something was off. He was still going too fast for a decent landing, and the wind shifted against his body. He looked up and saw his main canopy was misaligned. Keeping his breath steady, his heart rate ticked up. As a smoke jumper, he had experienced hard landings and knew this one wasn't going to be pretty. Upon impact, his left leg buckled and he tried to roll to the side in an attempt to avoid getting caught in the parachute cords. Agony washed over him once he stopped the forward motion, then everything went black.

He woke up in the hospital, in the ICU. He was told he was fresh from surgery to repair a compound fracture. On the first day, the doctors and nurses had said he was lucky to have survived. The compound break in his femur could have easily severed a major artery, and he had a fractured hip, punctured lung, and busted ribs. He was alive.

"Tric, wake up."

He bolted up, his heart hammering in his chest.

"Are you okay?" Kelly was crouched next to his chair. Concern filled her large gray eyes. She held his hand and applied comforting pressure. "Bad dream?"

"Something like that." He pushed himself to an upright position. "Sorry if I bothered you."

"It's fine. My boss is pretty easygoing."

Her attempt at lightening his mood didn't go unnoticed. He gave her a sleepy grin. "I must have drifted off."

She seemed to hesitate before standing. "Do you still want to go with me to the house?"

"Yeah, of course." He rubbed a hand over his eyes.

"I just need to wrap up a few things, and then we can leave when you're ready."

He rose to his feet, without the aid of his cane. "I'll be waiting."

*K*elly's heartbeat had finally returned to normal while she waited for her computers to shut down for the day. Was there more going on? An accident on the job wouldn't leave him with nightmares like what she had just witnessed, or the look of despair that lingered in his eyes.

When she walked out of her office, he was sitting on a kitchen stool, wearing an easygoing smile. The look that had been in his eyes just ten minutes earlier had dissipated like mist over the ocean.

"Let's hit the road." She grabbed her keys and locked the door, giving him plenty of room as he took the stairs one cautious step at a time. "Did you drive by the lighthouse when you were out today?" she asked.

"No. I drove along Shoreline Drive and then Main Street and back here."

She unlocked her Mini Cooper and got in. "How do you feel about convertibles?"

He grinned as he buckled his seat belt. "In January, normally not that great. But down here, we should go native."

She pushed a few buttons and waited for the top to fold back and down. She slid her dark sunglasses in place before backing out of the driveway. With a click of the radio, soon they were headed to Second Street, taking the long way to her place via the coastal route.

"This time of year, a few second homeowners come to the island, but mostly it's the year-round people who make up the population. We get to enjoy a slower pace of island life." She pointed to a building. "The Sandbar is planning a huge St. Patrick's Day event. If you're still here, you should come with me. They cook up some traditional dishes and the beer flows like water."

"Is it green?"

"Nope. The owner thinks that's sacrilegious, and unlike the Chicago River, we don't dump dye in the ocean for the additional festive touch."

"It sounds like fun. If I'm still here, I'll check it out."

He nodded as she continued to point out a few more places that he could go to catch a good meal. She slowed and turned onto her street. She didn't want to go back to what was left of her home, but she needed to check on the progress of rubble removal and she had an appointment with the contractor. It was time to finalize plans to rebuild. The only good thing was that she'd have her dream kitchen and would add the washer and dryer that hadn't been there before. She slowed as they approached her driveway. "I can't wait to get this behind me."

"Tonight or the construction project?"

"I hate not being in my own home." She parked in the driveway. "This is it. Home sweet home. Or it was."

In front of them a scorched cement pad and shrubs, with new posts rising straight up from freshly poured cement. She shuddered. "I just hate this." She heard the catch in her voice and wished she was stronger.

He touched her hand. "I know it's hard."

She pushed open her car door. "Do you want to walk

around or stay put?" She held her breath, surprised she wanted him to be with her.

"I'll come with you."

As they crossed the grass, she scuffed the ground with the toe of her canvas sneaker. "At least the debris is gone and I'm hopeful they can start rebuilding soon."

Tric walked around the foundation perimeter. "You said it was an electrical fire?"

"Yeah. By the time the fire alarms went off, the house was fully involved. They said with the age of the house, the wood was so dry it just went up."

"How old was the freezer?"

"It was new. I bought it off the mainland and when it was delivered, the guys pushed it in; they didn't carry it. The fire chief suspected something damaged the wiring and it just took time for the wires to get hot enough to burn." She shrugged. "I can't dwell on what was."

That made sense and there was nothing suspicious about that. He stopped in front of where the garage door had been. "Are you going to rebuild on the same footprint?"

"I am." In her mind's eye, she could see her home rise from the ashes. "But the interior will have a completely new layout. I know you can't see it from here, but from the living room, I could see a bit of the ocean. With the reconstruction, I'm going to have bigger windows on the second and third floors to take advantage of the view with the first floor the garage and storage areas. It's going to be awesome."

He leaned on his cane. "Sunshine always follows rain."

"Now you sound like my granny." Her heart felt lighter. He seemed to be a kindred spirit of Irish descent.

"It's just one of the many sayings I grew up with. I'm a

second-generation Irish American and in our family, we're very traditional, right down to a bunch of siblings who are starting to get married, so my mom and dad are looking forward to being grandparents."

"I have one brother, and my aunt and uncle stepped in for my parents. They passed a few years ago and my grandparents before that."

"I'm sorry to hear that."

"Thanks."

A pickup truck pulled in behind her Mini. "That's my contractor."

Tric moved off to the side. "I'll let you talk." He walked away, his gait slow but steady. She kept one eye on him, unsure how strong he really was. She had seen the pain etched around his mouth and she didn't want him tripping on something here. The last thing she needed was another accident on the property.

"Hey, Mike. It looks like we might be ready to roll."

He stuck out his hand. "Hi, Kelly. We're ready to start construction tomorrow."

"Awesome." She held up her hand and gave Mike a fist bump.

"You should plan on coming back Friday afternoon if possible and check out the progress. The framing will go fast."

She shook his hand. "It'll be hard for me to wait an entire week. But I'll try." She laughed and noticed Tric had made his way around the yard—not that it was a large lot, less than a quarter of an acre which was standard for the island.

"I'm gonna take off. See you next week." He hopped back in his truck and pulled away from the curb.

She closed her eyes and was imagining what it would

look like when she heard a groan and as she turned, she watched Tric stumble and fall. She raced over. "Are you okay?"

Through gritted teeth, he said, "I'm fine."

"What happened?" She held out her hand to help him.

"A wicked bad cramp and down I went."

She slipped an arm under his to keep him steady while he used the cane and heaved himself to a standing position. His cheeks flushed a deep shade of crimson, and he took a step away from her steadying hand.

Anxious to ease his discomfort, she said, "How about we pick up a pizza, drive out to the lighthouse, and have dinner on the beach? It's even deep-dish Chicago style."

"Comfort food from back home to distract me from kissing the ground and making a fool of myself?"

"No." Slowly, they made their way back to her car. "I'm starving and pizza on the beach near a lighthouse sounds good, and if we eat slow, we can watch the sunset."

"That's not something I can do in Chicago at this time of year." He eased into the passenger side while she got behind the wheel.

"How do you feel about extra cheese?" She backed the car around in the yard and waited for traffic to pass in front of them, lifting her hand to wave to a few of her neighbors. "If you're not a fan, we can do half and half."

"I love cheese and lots of toppings, so I say get the works."

She grinned. "Do you have any food allergies?"

"Nope."

"Then I'll order the local favorite."

He gave her a contemplative look. "My choice next time."

He was in for a treat and she pulled her phone from

her bag. "I'll call in for takeout so it will be ready when we get to the other side of the island."

"You're driving. I'm just along for the ride."

She flashed him a grin right before she placed their order. "Thanks. See you in a half hour." She disconnected. "Time to play tourist."

"Maybe tomorrow when I go out, I won't get lost."

She laughed. "It's an island. Keep going in circles and eventually you'll find your way home." That statement gave her a jolt. Her rental wasn't home for either one of them, just a temporary interlude. But what would it be like to have more with Tric, sharing more meals and afternoons like this? It was something she'd need to think about; after all, they had just met.

4

The lighthouse rose roughly one hundred feet above them. Tric tipped his head back. "The place has been decommissioned?"

Kelly smiled at the wonder in his voice. "Yes. With the new technology of protecting ships with radar and computers, this old lighthouse has become a part of history. It's withstood hurricanes and heaven knows what else, but it keeps standing like a sentinel protecting the island."

Kelly held out his cane, but he shook his head. "I'm good."

She carried the pizza box and he had the bag of sodas as they made their way to a picnic area in the shadow of the great structure. They sat side by side near a rocky outcropping to have a view of the ocean. The waves were rolling back with low tide.

"Do you like the ocean?" Kelly took a slice of the pizza, placed it on a paper plate the restaurant had provided, and handed it to Tric before she took a slice.

"I haven't spent much time near salt water. Lakes are

beautiful but not quite the same." Tric watched the waves while he inhaled the warm salty air deep into his lungs. It felt good to be able to take a deep breath. "There's nothing like being near the water but lake waves are much smaller. Doesn't the immense power make you feel small, almost insignificant? With each wave, the shore is washed clean."

She heard the wistfulness in his voice and wondered if he was hoping he could erase something as easily. "You haven't been through a hurricane yet—now that's power. I stayed through the last hurricane. It was only a category two but the intensity of being on this island at the height of the storm was a humbling experience. I think next time I'll go to the mainland. I'm a bit of a scaredy cat."

"Did you ride out the storm alone or go to a hurricane party? Those are a thing, right?"

She gave a small laugh. "I guess so, but I hunkered down at my place. I had only lived there a short time and like the captain of a ship, I was not abandoning it."

"That's pretty brave." He gave her a thoughtful look. "Or you're a touch crazy."

"I think it's the latter. After all, I've let a complete stranger stay in my home with me." What he didn't know was she'd checked him out on the internet and discovered he was exactly who he had said. Thankfully, she was a whiz at research too.

"I give you my word as a Scout, I'm harmless."

She cocked an eyebrow. "Were you?"

"All the way to Eagle Scout." He grinned. "So it counts."

"I'll think about that and get back to you. For now, we're good." A glob of warm cheese slid off the crust as she bit into it, and it landed on the sand. "Shoot. Melted cheese is the best part."

He was munching on his slice. "This isn't bad for Chicago-style pizza on an island."

"The owner is a transplant from up north. He's been here over thirty years but has the right touch when it comes to pizza. We'll have to try the seafood version next time instead of meat lovers."

"Next time? That sounds nice." He gave her a side-look. "Seafood on pizza? You're joking."

"Nope. It's a thing, and when you're surrounded by the ocean, it makes sense to enjoy fresh catch from the boat."

The minutes passed with pleasant conversation about the weather, food, and other easy topics. Curious, Kelly decided to dig deeper into this mystery man.

"I know you got hurt on the job, but what exactly happened?" She could see his face pale and hear his breath quicken. "Unless you don't want to talk about it."

*H*e looked away from her, down the beach where there were a few people jogging and a family walking a dog.

"I'm a firefighter." Well, that was true, but did she need to know he was a smoke jumper and chose to jump from a plane into an inferno? Most people didn't understand his profession and the satisfaction he extracted from living on the edge from June to October.

"That's how your uncle knows mine? He's a retired police officer," she said.

"Something like that." He felt a twinge of guilt. "But not exactly. The fire chief is my uncle and yeah, they've been friends for a long time. Both striving to protect and serve and being Irish, they seem to have an even closer bond."

"Did you work with your uncle?"

He sipped his cola. "No. I fight forest fires like you've seen on television that get out of control and people lose their homes and lives. For the last few years I've worked in Alaska, June to mid-October, but last year, it was cut short." He touched the cane handle. "And I'm still recovering."

Her eyes grew huge. "I've seen those fires on television. That's dangerous."

"Yes, it is. But someone needs to protect our forests; they're an essential part of our ecosystem." He tried to keep his tone of voice casual. He didn't mention being a smoke jumper; it was easier to let her think he worked on the line. But it was a huge adrenaline rush and he loved the men he spent months with. They had formed iron-clad relationships. They had each other's backs and they were closer than brothers when working, but during the off-months, they didn't have a lot of contact. Each respected that this time was precious. But most people couldn't understand why he chose that life.

"Now, going back to saying I'm a little crazy? We know who really is." She laughed and pointed a finger at him and then placed a hand on his arm.

He felt a shock of electricity race up it and jump-start his heart into a rhythm that he almost didn't remember and it felt nice. "Enough about me. Website programming. Sounds complex."

"Are you planning on going back?"

She wasn't going to drop the subject. "I'm not sure. It depends if I pass a physical, so for now, my career is on hold."

"I'm sorry. That has to be hard to be in limbo."

The kindness in her eyes told him she was sincere, and he felt the walls he had constructed around his heart start to crack. "I have to get back to Chicago and check in with the doctors sometime in March, so there's a slim chance I could return to work in June."

"Are you sure you want to keep doing it?"

He shrugged. "Good question, which is part of the reason I'm here—to figure out what I want to do for the next phase of my life."

She opened her mouth to ask another question and he shook his head. "Please, can you let it go for today?"

"Sure."

They finished eating the pizza in silence until she asked, "Do you want to go for a walk on the beach?"

Talking about his future had wiped him out emotionally and the ibuprofen he had taken before they left the beach house was beginning to wear off. "Can we do it another time? It's been a long day and I think the day is catching up to me. Do you mind if we call it a night?"

"Yeah, no prob." Kelly gathered up the garbage and tossed it into a barrel at the end of the picnic area. "Since we're still about a half hour before sunset, are you up for a quick drive around the rest of the island before heading home?"

He gave her a half smile. "Sounds good."

It did sound nice to just drive around, and it might help him get his bearings, even though given what she had said was true. On an island, you can always find your way home if you drive around in circles long enough.

· · ·

*L*earning that Tric got hurt on the job while battling a forest fire left Kelly with a thousand questions. She needed to respect his personal space and not come across like she was interrogating him, no matter how curious she was.

"Island living is great. During tourist season, you just wouldn't believe how many people we can cram onto a stretch of sand. People buy up houses and condos for rental income, but I love the space my house offers over the convenience of a condo." She joked to lighten the mood that had settled over the car. "What about you, apartment or a house in Chicago?"

"My family lives in Chicago so I use that as my home base, and I bought a condo a few years ago. It works out best for me since I'm gone for most of the summer, and if I had a house, who'd take care of the yard? When I'm home in the winter, shoveling isn't so bad; it helps to keep me moving. Someday I'll have a house, when I decide to have kids."

"Anyone special in your life?" She felt her cheeks flame hot. "Sorry. I tend to be a little too inquisitive for my own good." She flashed him a sympathetic smile. "We can trade sob stories if you want. If you have one, I mean."

Tric finally grinned. "I think those might be stories over a beer or glass of good Irish whiskey—that is, if you have any back at the house."

"What kind of good Irish lass would I be if I didn't have a wee drop every now and then?"

Tric's smile grew even wider if that was possible and it warmed her heart. "Are you a good enough Irishwoman to actually hold your liquor?"

With a jab to his shoulder, she said, "Maybe you're not

enough of an Irishman to hold yours. So be careful, Mr. Ryan. This lady might just show you a thing or two."

"You are a wee bit of a sassy Irish lass and I like it," he answered with a thick accent. She liked how he could slip into an authentic brogue and wondered if he had spent time there. "You sound just like my gran."

She laughed. "Tonight, we sip and savor." She slowed the car at the edge of the pier, as close as she could get to the water's edge and still stay in the car. "Just in time for sunset."

Quietly, Kelly sat and peeked at Tric from out of the corner of her eye. He was a good-looking guy and seemed nice, so why wasn't he here with a girlfriend instead of escaping to the beach alone?

Without looking at her, he said, "I can almost hear your wheels spinning with all kinds of questions."

She pointed to the horizon. "Shh, you don't want to miss the exact moment the sun kisses the water; it's slow and sweet until the moment she gives in and slips out of sight."

His voice deepened. "You make it sound like lovers embracing."

She was transfixed. It didn't matter how many times she sat and watched; it made her heart ache just a little that the day had come to an end, but tomorrow would be a new beginning. Would Tric understand the fresh possibilities that were mere hours away?

The sky was a gradient peach above the sinking sun and the horizon a deep orange. The white caps were tinged with a pale pink and the beach had deepening purple shadows. As night fell, the darkness enveloped the car and the spectacular show was over for another day.

Tric broke the comforting silence. "That was beautiful. I

don't know if I've ever seen a sky with so many shades of orange, and the few high clouds were almost purple."

"I love coming out here at any time of the year."

"How do you feel about sunrises?"

"I'm not much of a morning person, but there are days when I go on the kitchen deck and watch it." She glanced his way. "You'll have to do that before you head home."

"Yeah."

She gave a slight shiver. Now that the sun had gone down, the cool air was rapidly setting in. She pushed the button for the top and it clicked into place.

"How about that drink now?"

"Sounds good," Tric said. "Thanks for bringing me out here tonight."

She felt a crooked smile slide over her face. "You're welcome." She eased from the parking area and headed back to their side of the island.

5

*W*hen they got back to Shamrock Cottage, Tric sat in a lounge chair next to Kelly on the deck overlooking the shadow-filled beach.

He soaked in the ambience Kelly had created with a few lit candles and the kitchen light casting a soft glow across the floor.

He took a sip of his whiskey. "This is smooth."

"After a busy day, I think the best thing to do is watch the water and, now that I'm staying here, sip a beverage that tastes better in crystal." She smiled and took another sip.

"It's a pretty sight." But in that moment, he wasn't looking at the horizon; he was looking at the beautiful woman sitting next to him and he didn't even care if it was a cliché. It had been an exhausting day despite the snooze during the afternoon. Tomorrow he'd get out and walk the beach and try to find a place to work out.

"Hey, where did you go?"

Her voice tugged him out of his thoughts. "Making a plan for tomorrow."

"Making plans." She waited for a couple of moments.

He chuckled. "Yeah, I guess I just left that hanging. Sorry. I need to find a place where I can focus on upper body workouts and I'm going to start clocking some miles on the beach. I figure walking on the sand will help me get stronger." He tapped his thigh. "I have to start rebuilding my strength."

"I walk in the mornings before work, if you want company." She didn't look at him but watched the moon begin to rise. She held up her hand and tilted her head toward the water. "Listen."

They sat in the quiet. He wasn't sure what they were listening for. An ice cream truck coming down the street or the garbage man?

Nothing but simple silence. She leaned her head back against the cushions and closed her eyes, a small smile gracing her lush lips.

"Kelly, what are we waiting to hear?"

"I'm just remembering the moment when the sun met the horizon. Did you know if you listen really hard when the sun kisses the water, the day sighs, but when the moon comes up, it's in silence? It has completed all it needed to do and tomorrow is a brand-new chance to live life again. I think it was Ralph Waldo Emerson who said, 'Every sunset brings the promise of a new dawn.'"

"I never thought of it as a new beginning, only the end of what had been." He grew thoughtful. Is that where he was in his life, on the edge of a new beginning? It was hard to say, as his future depended on his physical recovery.

The shadows slipped around the deck and lights from the neighbors illuminated part of the street that bordered the beach.

LUCINDA RACE

"It's peaceful here." His voice was soft so as not to break the moment. She was right; the sunset had been magical.

"As much as I love my house, I'm going to miss this view when I move home. There's nothing like it on the island."

"Did you think about selling after the house is rebuilt and buying something closer to the water?"

"Too expensive, and I do love living in the middle of the island too. It gives me a reason to hop on my bike and take a ride."

"Sounds fun." He drained the last of his whiskey. "Kel, thanks for making today normal and not treating me different."

Her eyebrows shot up. "What are you talking about?"

"When I was back home, everyone wanted to help me —drop off meals, or my sister would come over to visit and would clean my house. It was like everyone thought I was fragile."

"You had major surgery and if you've been recovering since—what did you say?—September? My guess is you needed a bit of help. Besides, you know how family is, especially ones that have some Irish in the blood. Always wanting to help."

He knew she was right about how long he had been recovering, but was he ever going to be the man he was before the fateful jump?

"If you were serious about me tagging along in the morning, what time do you leave?" he asked.

"Seven. I can tap on your door before I leave. You can go as far as you want."

"How long are you gone?"

36

"About an hour but I'm not a jogger, just a walker, and we can take it at your pace."

"I don't want to hold you up, so if I'm too slow, you can go on ahead."

She waved a hand at him. "We don't need to worry about all this tonight. We'll take it as it comes."

He slid to the edge of the lounge chair and, using his cane for leverage, heaved himself up. To her credit, Kelly never asked if she could help him, but he could feel her watching him.

"Thanks for the invite and I'll take you up on it, but for now I'm going to turn in." He hoped she wouldn't judge him and think nine was too early, but she didn't seem to.

"Sleep well."

He hobbled into the kitchen and then thought better of taking a pill; he had been drinking and they didn't mix. Instead, he saw a bottle of aspirin and tossed back a couple with a swallow of water, then he made his way, in slow, labored steps, to his bedroom. He couldn't wait to stretch out. Hopefully sleep would be quick and dreamless.

*O*nce she was alone, Kelly exhaled a ragged breath. That man was hurting not just physically but to his core, and if anything could help, it was this beach. She hadn't realized how much pain he was still in or she wouldn't have offered up her special whiskey. He probably needed a pain pill more than a touch of their Irish roots. But she didn't need to micromanage what he drank; he was a big boy and could make up his own mind.

She sat in the semidarkness and thought about rebuilding her home. It was going to be fun picking out cabinets and bath fixtures. Even given a choice, she would stay on the island; she had a sense of peace she didn't get anywhere else. She could forget and maybe even forgive Harry for breaking her heart. But ten years wasn't long enough to want to go home to Boston and let him make amends.

When goosebumps raced over her arms, it was time to head inside. In a few short months, the humidity would drive her in. Funny how the weather dictated how she lived her life. Most people would think she'd be outside all year around here, but with air conditioning beckoning on the worst days, it was a good escape. A thought flitted through her brain. Maybe Last Chance Beach was her escape even now.

~

The next morning, Kelly tapped on Tric's bedroom door. Not hearing any movement, she tiptoed down the hall in stocking feet. Maybe he had decided to sleep in instead of hitting the beach. She was thinking about the website design she was going to work on today for a new candy store. It was expanding into online sales and her plan was to have the chocolates jump off the page while making the customer feel like they were in the store shopping.

When she walked into the kitchen, Tric was sitting at the breakfast bar. He wore a wide grin and a baseball cap that matched his workout tee and loose-fitting shorts. He was a handsome guy but she held her reaction in check when she saw the red, angry-looking scar on his lower leg and could only guess the one on his upper thigh was worse.

"Good morning. I wondered when you were going to

SHAMROCKS ARE A GIRL'S BEST FRIEND

come out of your room." He picked up his sunglasses and handed her a stainless steel water bottle. "Here you go."

She took it. "Thanks. What time did you get up?"

"About forty-five minutes ago. I think you're right about this place; I slept great and I think that's why I'm feeling strong today."

She noticed his face was unlined from pain and his eyes were bright. "Then I guess we should get walking."

He picked up his cane. "My goal is to walk without using it."

"This is your first time, so don't push it. We can turn around when you've had enough." She held open the door and after he stepped out on the back deck, she locked it. It was a spectacular morning. The sun was bright; the tang of the salty air teased her nose, and the breeze was light. Kelly loved this time of day.

"Are you going to be comfortable dressed in yoga pants and your tee?"

"They're exercise gear so they wick away moisture. I can get away with stuff like this until the humidity and temperatures skyrocket closer to triple digits."

Side by side, they descended the wide wooden steps to the cement parking area.

"It's rare to hit one hundred, but we'll come close in July." She adjusted her ballcap, tightened her ponytail, and looked at him through large round sunglasses. She could swear his eyes roamed over her body, but his own dark glasses prevented her from really knowing where he was looking. She perked up at the idea that he might like what he saw.

She pointed to a walkway from the edge of the road which led up and over to the beach. They crossed the ocean front street and she noticed he was taking his time, placing one foot in front of the other, but there was no sign of discomfort on his face, and now she was glad he couldn't tell where she was looking. She didn't want to make him feel self-conscious about his injuries or that she was really checking him out, but his backside was a pretty good view too, and she blushed as she looked away so he wouldn't catch her staring.

Tric gingerly stepped onto the sand and flashed her a tentative grin. "I'm determined to soak up the magic of this beach."

She guided him down to the hard-packed sand. The tide was going out. "Want to go right or left?"

"Ladies' choice." He was watching the water and pointed farther out. "Look. Do you think that is a dolphin or a shark?"

"More like a large fish. We've never had shark sightings for as long as I've been here. Now, I know they're out there, but it's not something I dwell on." She shuddered just thinking about what might be closer to the shore than she cared to admit.

"The ocean is like a huge door to the unknown, at least to us landlubbers."

"Exactly. I'll never be one to go exploring in the depths." She touched his arm. "Let's go right."

Before they could start, her cell rang. "I just want to see who this is." Kelly pulled it from her pocket. "It's my uncle. Maybe he's found you a place to stay." She swiped to accept the call. "Hi, Uncle Kevin, what's going on?"

"Hey, Kelly. I'm afraid I have some bad news. I can't find Tric a new rental. Would it be okay if he continued to share the house with you?"

Her heart skipped in her chest. "Like for the next two months?"

She smiled as her uncle chuckled. "That's the idea. No vacancies mean no rooms."

"It's okay with me but I'll talk it over with Tric and let you know." She disconnected and put the phone in her pocket. "Well, I've got news. Not sure if you're going to think it's good or bad."

"Go on." He paused.

"My uncle can't find a new rental for you and he asked if it'd be okay if you stayed with me."

His lips slanted down. "I'll just pack up and head home."

She kicked the sand with the toe of her sneaker. "Tric, I'm good with you staying here until the end of your trip. The house is big enough for the two of us to share. Heck, it's big enough for twelve people."

A smile tipped his lips and then broadened. "Are you sure?"

She gave him a nod, which made her ponytail bounce. "Absolutely." She held up her hand. "Roomies?"

He slapped her a high five. "Roomies."

The jolt made her knees knock.

He touched the rim of her ballcap. "How do you catch a school of fish?"

"With a net?"

He chuckled. "Bookworms."

She gave him a playful poke in his side and he laughed. "I'm starting to see how you think you're funny, but you're going to need to work on your jokes."

He rubbed his hands together. "I'm just warming up."

"I'll keep that in mind." His corny jokes were funny, and she liked that he was trying to make things easy between them. With any luck, the next two months would be as easy as the first two days.

6

---

*A*s Tric and Kelly climbed the stairs to the cottage, there was no way he was going to tell her he was as tired as the wings on a bird. On the sly, he glanced at his phone. It had only been thirty-five minutes since they hit the beach. Six months ago, he would have run for at least an hour, and today, what amounted to a morning stroll had exhausted him.

"Do you have plans?" Kelly turned the key in the lock and they entered the sunny kitchen.

He perched on the edge of a stool, taking the pressure off his throbbing leg. "Do you mean at this very minute, or is that a general question about the overall goal for the day?" He smiled as she twirled the ends of her ponytail around her finger.

"You know I mean in the general sense, and stop poking at your new roomie." She pushed the on button for the coffee maker and withdrew two mugs and small glasses. "Juice?"

"Please." He took the glass of OJ she passed to him and

withdrew the pill bottle from his pocket and then changed his mind. "I'm going to take ibuprofen."

She gave him a quizzical look before taking a bottle from the cabinet and handing it to him.

"Thanks. I want to wean off the meds and just use over-the-counter stuff, and if I need something stronger, I'll use it at night."

"You're really challenging yourself today. The walk and now this."

He knew she might think he was crazy but today, while walking on the beach, something had cracked open inside of him. She had been right. Last Chance Beach was just the place to start over, whatever that might mean.

He threw back a couple of pills with the juice and forced a grin on his face. "Now, you were asking me about my plans."

The coffee pot sputtered. Kelly's hand hovered over the handle, and then she filled the mugs. "You're keeping me in suspense." She glanced up through her lashes and it was then he noticed how large her eyes were. He could spend the morning just looking into them. The laughter and warmth that hovered almost felt like an invitation to fun.

"Right. How about I make dinner tonight? What's your favorite meal?" Tric asked.

"You don't have to do that. We can cook together."

"I'd like to do this for you, so tell me what your favorite dish is."

She tapped her chin. "If I could have anything at all, it'd be oysters on the half shell." She wrinkled her nose. "Nah. Sushi? Not in the mood."

She pursed her lips, and damn, she was cute. Not that he could make sushi, and oysters were not his thing unless his mom made her famous Irish oysters cooked with bacon, cabbage, and Guinness hollandaise, but that was a holiday treat.

"In all honesty, my favorite meal is my mother's Irish stew and soda bread." She got a faraway look in her eye. "Growing up, Mom would make Grandma's recipe with lamb and there was always homemade bread."

"What made it so good?"

"The lamb and chunks of potatoes and carrots simmered in the broth all afternoon really got the mouth watering, and the bread was so tender."

He could call his mom for a recipe or maybe do one better. Could he track down the family recipe through her uncle? He was a pretty good cook, and it would be a nice surprise for her. The bread he already knew how to make, but it was his granny's recipe. It would be like blending their families through food, but maybe she'd think he was being presumptuous so he'd keep that thought to himself.

"Then mashed potatoes and meatloaf it is."

She flashed him a smile and snorted. "Don't forget gravy without lumps." She picked up her coffee. "I'm going to shower and get ready for work." Her brow arched, the concern was evident in her eyes. "Are you good?"

"Yeah. I'm going to enjoy my coffee on the deck and get cleaned up too. See you at lunch."

She went into her office and then came right back. Handing him the newspaper, she said, "There are a few gyms listed on the mainland if you wanted to check them out."

"Thanks." He glanced down and saw she had circled one. With a smile and a wink, she turned and went into her bedroom.

He waited until the door closed and the sound of the shower running in her bathroom indicated the coast was clear. He called the chief, who answered on the third ring.

After exchanging the normal pleasantries and an update on his recovery, he said, "I guess you heard what happened with the cottage?"

"Yeah, Kevin called to fill me in."

"I was hoping you could help me out. I want to make dinner for Kelly tonight and she said her favorite meal was her grandmother's Irish stew. Since she's agreed to let me stay here, I want to do something nice."

"Tric, why don't you just fix the stew you already know how to make?"

"If you'd seen the look on her face when she talked about her granny's stew, you'd know why, but I'm baking my soda bread."

The chief chuckled. "Now you're talking. Too bad I wasn't in the neighborhood. I'd swing by."

"So you'll help me?"

"Only if you promise when you get back to town, you'll hook me up with bread and stew."

Tric grinned and shook his head. "You got it."

"Give me about a half hour and I should be able to have just what you need."

"Thanks." He set the phone on the counter and carefully stood up, knowing he might be stiff after the walk, but it wasn't too bad. After filling up his mug, he grabbed a muffin and his phone off the counter and headed out to the deck. He kept his phone out so he wouldn't miss the chief's call. He'd never let him down.

. . .

*W*ith his cane under one arm, Tric's mood was light as he walked up the stairs carrying two large shopping bags filled with ingredients to make Kelly's granny's famous Irish stew, his gran's soda bread, and he even picked up some Guinness. He only hoped he'd do the stew justice. Every cook's dish always came out slightly different than the original version, but in this case he hoped it was the thought that counted.

After putting the groceries away, he went to the deck and stretched out for a bit to take the pressure off his leg. He drifted off to sleep and woke with a start. Feeling better, he started whistling an old Irish song. He turned the oven on to preheat. He wanted to get the bread in the oven before he started the main meal. But what of dessert? He should have thought of that in the store but maybe he could whip something up? A Guinness chocolate cake? If all else failed, he knew the cake would be a winner.

He heard her office door open and he stumbled as he moved to block her view of the counter by leaning against it. "Hey, Kel. What's up?" Damn, that hurt, but he kept his face neutral so she wouldn't come in the kitchen.

How quickly he had moved to shortening her name, but based on her smile, she didn't seem to mind.

"I heard you banging around out here and was curious." She tried to look around him and he moved to dodge her efforts, frustrated he moved so slowly. With a mischievous sparkle in her eye, she said, "I'm guessing our meal is top secret until tonight?"

He gave a single nod and a smile that grew from one side of his face to the other. "Now, do me a favor. If you're dying for a drink or something, just shoot me a text or yell and I'll bring it to you."

With an assessing look, she tipped her head to the side, hesitating. "How about a compromise? I'll meet you halfway so you're not running around waiting on me. After all, you are making me a home-cooked meal which is very sweet."

He bobbed his head from side to side. "Play your cards right and there might even be dessert tossed in."

"Ah ha. So... you stopped at the bakery. Even better."

He cocked an eyebrow. There was one thing he was going to have to educate the beautiful Kelly about. His homemade cake was way better than anything from a bakery.

"Something like that." He pointed to her office. "You're hereby banished for the next"—he glanced at the wall clock above the kitchen window—"well, until at least five."

She grinned. "In that case, a snack, water, and a bio break."

He grinned. "If you must, but be quick about it."

Over her shoulder, she laughed. "I could definitely get used to this."

He continued to lean against the counter so when she came out of the bathroom, she wouldn't be able to see anything. He wasn't sure what had gotten into him to make him feel so spunky, but the playful banter with her was just good fun. It had been a long time since he had felt this carefree and relaxed.

His thoughts drifted to Alyssa, the woman he had believed would someday be his wife. It had been hard on her to be in a relationship with a man who was gone for months at a time, risking his life to put out wildfires. Her greatest fear was that he'd return home broken or worse, and she had ended it over a year ago. Funny how her fear had become his reality. He was broken in lots of places. Taking a deep breath, he was pleased to discover he could do that without a twinge of discomfort. Part of him had healed. Now to get the leg back in running form.

Kelly popped back into the hall and pretended to pout. "Are you waiting on me so I won't see what you're up to?"

"Yup. Now back to work and you'll get office delivery."

She laughed over her shoulder. "I like ice in my glass of tea."

"Who said you're getting iced tea?"

"With lemon," came the muffled response.

A soft tap on Kelly's office door drew her attention away from the screen. She glanced at the clock. It was almost six. "Come in."

Tric stuck his head in the door. "Dinner's ready whenever you want to eat."

Stretching her arms overhead, she eased out of the chair. "I lost track of time."

He waved for her to follow him. "You must be hungry."

She stepped out of her office, paused, then hurried down the hall. "Is that stew I smell?"

His smile was wide as he moved slowly into the kitchen.

When she reached the spacious room, she stopped in her tracks. The table was set for two, with a small bouquet of wildflowers in the center. "What did you do all afternoon?" This was seriously sweet. No one had never gone to this much trouble for her.

"I read a book, did a little cooking, and relaxed." He

crossed his arms and wore a bemused smile on his face. He whisked out a chair. "Are you interested in joining me?"

She threw her arms around him in an impulsive hug. Tric stumbled back and his breath caressed her cheek. "Thank you for all of this." She slid onto her chair, taking in the table from the cloth napkins to the flowers. It felt like a date but better. This was totally unexpected. "I can't wait to dig in."

He put a Dutch oven in the middle of the table and left the cover on. Her mouth began to water. He placed a cloth-covered breadbasket and the butter dish on the table, poured a half glass and set it and a bottle of beer next to her plate. His eyes twinkled. "I hope you like Guinness."

She grinned. "Am I Irish?"

With a grand gesture, he removed the pot lid. "For your dining pleasure, I present Granny O'Malley's famous stew."

With a laugh, she asked, "How did you get Granny's secret recipe?"

He held a finger to his lips. "Top secret. I hope I did it justice."

Even if dinner was tasteless, this would be one of the best meals of her life. Tric was a man filled with surprises.

She ladled stew into her bowl and dipped her spoon into the gravy, tasting it. "Tric, this is amazing. It tastes just like I remember."

"I'm glad, but save room for dessert. I baked a cake."

"I have one question." She closed her eyes and savored a spoonful of potato and carrot. When she opened her eyes, she looked him square in his. "Marry me?"

His mouth gaped open and he said with utmost seriousness, "Don't you think we should kiss first?"

She waved her spoon over her bowl and then encompassed the table. "This is all I need to know."

"Well, in that case, you might want to taste the cake before I answer." He gave her a wink. "Just to be sure."

After they were done with the main course, Kelly cleaned up the dishes while Tric sliced the chocolate cake and poured a finger of whiskey into two glasses. They were going to have dessert on the deck and watch the sunset.

"Tric, thank you again for dinner tonight. I know it took a lot of effort to put this all together and you must be exhausted, but it was delicious and reminded me of sitting with my family at Granny's house."

"You miss them." It wasn't a question but a statement.

"I do, but tonight Boston didn't seem so far away." She gave him a grateful smile.

"It's the least I can do. I showed up in your living room and you took pity on me, giving me shelter and the encouragement to start walking and exercising again. I know it's what I had to do but you're a good person and better than I could have expected, so thank you."

He handed her a glass and tapped his to hers. She said, "To new friends."

7

a few days had passed since Tric made dinner for
Kelly, and they had fallen into an easy routine.
The magic of Last Chance Beach seemed to be hard at
work. They walked each morning on the beach, and he
was getting stronger and only using the cane when he was
very tired. On Friday morning they enjoyed breakfast
together, and then she disappeared into her office. He
planned to spend a couple of hours working out at a gym
on the mainland. His muscles were sore but in a good way,
and following the plan the physical therapist had made up
for him was starting to pay off.

Later that morning, after a tough workout and before
heading back to the cottage, he made a detour to pick up
sandwiches for their lunch. He tapped his fingers on the
steering wheel in time to Brooks and Dunn. There was
nothing like a little foot-stomping country music to put a
smile on his face.

He slowed as he drove past her house and was pleased
to see the exterior walls were going up and it was starting
to take shape. Maybe Kelly would want to run over

LUCINDA RACE

tonight and check it out for herself, or even tomorrow. He pulled into the sandwich shop's parking lot.

Like a date? If he had met her back home, he would have asked her out, but was it weird since they were living together? Dinner had been kind of like a date. All that had been missing was the kiss good night. Sitting under the stars with her over dessert had given his heart a tug or three.

With his mind made up, he walked into the Sand Dollar Café and ordered roast beef and turkey sandwiches, chips, lemonade, and two giant chocolate chip cookies for later. He was ready to head for home.

Kelly peered into the refrigerator, wondering what she could have for lunch. The stew was gone and cake was an option, but a tiny part of her felt guilty eating sweets for lunch. Shouldn't there be some protein or something green on her plate?

The sound of footsteps on the stairs put a smile on her face and she stood up. Tric walked in, his cane looped over his arm, carrying a bag with the SD Café logo on the front and a cardboard tray with cups sporting water beads from the heat of the day. Could there be something in there for her?

He held up the bag. "I brought lunch. Are you interested?"

"Yes, but I'm dying to get out of the house. Want to eat on the beach?"

"I was hoping you'd suggest lunch alfresco."

She noticed something was different, and then it dawned on her. "You're not using your cane?"

"I'm feeling stronger and trying not to be dependent on

it. You're right about this place; it has amazing restorative powers, almost like magic."

He had no idea that, in fact, this place was supposed to be full of magic, to heal bodies, hearts, and souls. Last Chance Beach changed everything. Taking the bag, she stepped into flip-flops and grabbed her sunglasses. "Ready."

*S*itting on the blanket in the sand, Kelly stretched her legs out in front of her and wiggled her toes. The sun was high in the cloudless deep-azure sky and the breeze wafted over the water. She inhaled a lungful of the fresh salt air.

"If I could figure out a way to work on a computer while sitting on the beach, I would. The combination of sun, air, and sand is perfect." She shaded her eyes and noticed Tric was watching the water with a mellow expression on his face. Even though she wore her sunglasses, the glare off the sand was intense. "What are you thinking about?"

"Just enjoying the moment. In my real world, I never take time to just relax in the middle of the day. This place has a nice appeal."

"Tell me about the life of being a firefighter."

He looked over the water. "It's hard work, and being on the front lines is dangerous most of the time. My old girlfriend said I was an adrenaline junkie."

"But to put yourself on the line and try to save a home or a business is heroic in my eyes."

He looked in the opposite direction. "I'm not that kind of firefighter. I'm a smoke jumper."

That almost sounded like a confession, and she gave

him a long look, but she wasn't about to confess she already knew. "Aren't those the men and women who jump out of a plane to fight forest fires, like on the West Coast?"

"And Alaska." He tapped his chest. "That's where I work most of the time."

"Wow." She couldn't think of anything else to say.

"Change your mind on the hero thing and moved on to crazy?" He gave her a sidelong look.

"I'm not sure what to think, other than that sounds freaking scary."

"The jumping out of planes or fighting fires with the tools on your back?"

"Both." She lay back on the blanket and looked up at the seagulls flying overhead. "So, when you got hurt last fall, you were fighting a fire. How did you get out?"

"Yeah, it was a jump gone wrong. I was ported part of the way down the trail until a helicopter could get in and pick me up."

"That sounds awful." Her stomach lurched when she thought of his pain. It had to have been unbelievable to be injured so badly that he was still recovering.

"Wasn't my best day. On the upside, I'm a walking hardware store." He gave her a crooked smile. "I'll recover."

She hesitated to ask, but said, "Will you go back to being a smoke jumper?"

"I'm not sure if I can. You have to be in peak physical condition and with the extent of these injuries, I might not be back to one hundred and ten percent, which is the requirement. If you're not strong, you're the weak link, and that means so many things can go sideways fast."

"But you're working hard at the gym." Her feelings

had gone from admiration to worry to downright concern for him. What if he was pushing himself too hard? She was surprised that she was already feeling connected to him in a very different way than just casual friends.

"I've had to accept that might not be enough. I think I mentioned that in March, I have to go back and have a physical. That will indicate if I'm headed back to the team or finding a new career. If I have any doubt, I'll step aside."

He stated the facts but underneath it all, she could hear his bubbling emotions. He loved his job but his injuries had been life-altering, maybe in more ways than even he understood. Sometimes fate steps in and makes a person take a hard look at life; maybe this was Tric's time for reflection.

"If you pass, when do you go back to the line?"

"June. And before you ask if I don't, I'm not sure what I'll do next. In past off-seasons, I've hung out at the local firehouse, which is how I became good friends with a bunch of traditional firefighters under my uncle's command."

Softly, she said, "All roads lead back to home."

"I've been thinking about what might be next and I'm still coming up blank. I thought briefly about a city fireman but if I can't pass the test for my current job, I won't pass the other test to work in a more traditional fire-house." He leaned forward and touched her hand. "Don't look so down. I'll be fine. I'm strong and stubborn. If I'm not fighting forest fires, I'll figure out something."

"Well, thank you for working to save our forests." She regretted the words, thinking they sounded trite.

"You're welcome, and for the record, you're the first person to ever say that to me."

She sat up and touched his good leg. "I meant it."

Tric continued to watch her for what seemed like forever. Finally, he said, "What are you doing tomorrow?"

"Cleaning, which you get to help with. Laundry, and I'm not sure what else. Why?"

"How would you like to spend the day playing tourist with me? And in full transparency, I mean a date, not just two people hanging out."

Without hesitation, she said, "I'd like that on one condition—we end up at Rod's. It has great food and cold beverages."

"I love local places."

"Do you have something specific you want to do tomorrow?"

"I saw a flyer about historic tours and a dolphin watch out of the marina. There's a sailboat leaving at two, and it's out for a couple of hours. We could do that and then go to an early dinner and maybe catch sunset on the beach if we make it in time."

Her heart skipped when she thought of going on a date with him, and all that it might imply. "I never did a boat tour. It sounds like fun."

His eyes grew wide. "You've lived on the island how long? How could you not have done the tour?"

She held up a hand. "In my defense, I don't think locals typically do the tourist stuff. I mean, how many things have you done back home that a tourist would want to do?"

He gave a snort. "Point taken."

Her phone pinged and she looked at the screen. "I have to get back to the office. One of my clients is panicked. She sent the wrong text for her sale and the wrong information is live." She hopped up and brushed off her backside, disappointed lunch ended abruptly.

*T*ric got to his feet and stumbled before catching himself. His leg was cramped up and he flexed and bent it, trying to work out the kink.

A flash of concern crossed her face. "What's wrong?"

"Nothing. Just a twinge. It's no big deal." He wanted to get back to the house and chill for a while. He had to make a full recovery. There was no other option.

They picked up the trash and carried it to the garbage can. Kelly kept peeking at him from the corner of her eye. "Are you sure you're fine?"

"Absolutely." He wanted to take her hand but wasn't sure it was the right time. For now, they were in the friend zone. Tomorrow would be the date zone. The timing might be better then.

"This was a nice break. Thanks for suggesting it." She gave him a sunny smile that dimmed the sun. "Now it's back to work."

"I'm going to hang on the deck and catch up on a little reading. Earlier, I picked up an older Dan Brown novel."

Her gaze flitted to his leg. "Good idea. I was going to order pizza for dinner."

They really were sharing a lot over the last few days and he could feel his attraction to her growing. But where was this going to go? If he was going home and back to his life, he'd have to leave her behind, so he needed to keep things casual between them even if his heart disagreed with his head. "Pizza sounds good." He gave her a wink. "Maybe we can try the seafood version this time."

$\mathcal{W}$hile Kelly worked, Tric stretched out on the lounge chair with his laptop and the novel he picked up. He needed to check email and pay a few bills before he started to read. As he scrolled through the junk mail clogging his inbox, he saw a couple of emails from his team leader. He clicked on the first one. It was checking in on his recovery. The second was much of the same, and the third made his mouth go dry. It had the date for his physical, the week before St. Patrick's Day. His heart sank. Deep down, he had doubts he would pass. It was still weeks away and if he wasn't going to be able to take his spot with the unit, they'd have to fill it. Time was needed to train a new person and he understood, but it was hard to think of not returning to the job he loved.

He wrote a short reply that rehab was going well and he would be back in Chicago in time for the physical. As a final note, he asked if there was an opportunity to get back on his team for the following year if he wasn't ready. Teams typically stayed together for years, and if he didn't get back to his team, there would be a new guy to take his place. He hesitated but didn't erase the question and hit send. The chances would be slim if he didn't get back there this year. If that was the case, what would he want to do with his life? It was a question he kept asking himself, but he had yet to find an answer. The only thing he had ever done was fight wildfires.

Going back to college was an option, but his mind was blank with what he would study. He picked up his cell phone.

On the second ring, his uncle answered. "Tric, how the heck are ya?"

"Doing good. Beach life is pretty close to perfect." He turned to look into the kitchen and gave a wave to Kelly, who was getting something to drink. "And the scenery is great."

"You're feeling better?"

"Yup. I'm working out at the gym and walking on the beach every day and the cane is becoming an occasional tool."

"That is good news. So what else is going on?"

"I got an email with the date for my physical for work, and it's right before St. Patrick's Day. I'm worried I won't pass."

"Ah, Tric. You have plenty of time to rebuild your strength. Don't count yourself out yet."

"I have to be realistic. Which is why I'm calling. If I fail, what do you think about becoming a Chicago firefighter? Is there a chance I could use my experience and get a job at the station?" He knew the answer but threw it out there anyway.

"To be a CFD member, you need to be an EMT and pass an exhaustive physical which is different than what you're doing now, but it's not out of reach. What if you became an instructor?"

"And be on the fringe while everyone is out slaying a fire-breathing dragon?" Just thinking about sitting on the sidelines was like ash in his mouth.

"Your injuries were severe, and although it's not impossible, I would encourage you to think about all your options. What kind of uncle would I be if I didn't?"

Tric knew he was right. "I'll give it some thought, and I appreciate the straight talk."

"I'll do some checking around and see if I can find any information on instructor training if you want, but no pressure."

"Thanks. I'll swing by the station when I get back to town."

"Stop in around dinnertime and you can hang out with the guys. Heck, we might even put you to work peeling potatoes."

With a snort, he said, "You just want me to cook. I know how this works."

"You're one of the best firehouse cooks around. Alright, Tric, I need to get back to the stack of paperwork on my desk, but I'll see you in a few weeks."

"Take it easy." He put the phone aside and closed his computer. The chief had given him something to mull over —teaching. It wasn't as exciting as being on the front line, but it was an option.

He closed his eyes and enjoyed being outside in February. He couldn't do this back home.

· · ·

*K*elly wondered who Tric was talking to on the phone. He frowned a lot and was shaking his head when she went back into her office. She knew he was at a crossroads and after she had looked up the description of smoke jumpers, she was in awe of his courage to walk into an inferno with only his wits, team, and the tools he carried in. He was a brave man.

~

*T*he next day was Tric's first date with Kelly. He looked in the mirror and noticed he needed a haircut and should have gotten one before heading south. He checked his watch. It was just after twelve thirty, so he strolled into the kitchen. He was pleasantly surprised to see she was waiting for him.

"Hey, pokey." Her smile warmed her pretty eyes. "What took you so long?"

He patted the top of his head. "Bad hair day." He deliberately fluttered his eyelashes and then chuckled. "Monday, I'll get a haircut."

"Good thing one of us is having a good hair day." She stood up and squeezed his hand.

That now familiar thrill raced through his veins. He leaned in and brushed her cheek, but his lips hovered there. "You look great."

She smoothed a hand over her floral print shirt and deep-purple skort. He couldn't help but notice that her long, toned legs seemed to go on for miles and her hair was pulled off her face in a clip.

He said, "I booked the boat for two. Should we just head to the marina?"

"There are some shops we can check out while we wait to board, so let's head there."

"I'll drive."

She said, "We'll take the Mini. It's easier to park than your huge SUV, but you can drive if you can handle a stick?" She tossed the keys in his direction and he grabbed them.

"I think the leg's ready to handle it and it's been a while, but tooling around in your car is fun. Thank heavens the seats go back far enough for comfort."

Her eyes crinkled when she laughed. "Most people think the car is best for the vertically challenged but it's surprisingly roomy as long as you don't have any backseat passengers."

He gestured to the door. "Are you ready?"

She took the house keys from the dish on the counter. "Now I am."

With a toss of her long hair, they got into the car and he put the top down. "Is turning left the fastest route?"

"No. Go right." She adjusted her sunglasses. "That's the quickest route and we can avoid some of the Saturday traffic."

With a quick right, he made it to the marina within twenty minutes. After the drive, he said, "You were right. This was the best way to go." He eased into a parking spot and frowned while he looked for the button to put the top up and then was happy when it began to move. "I'm really looking forward to the sailboat."

As they got out, he looked over the roof of the car. "The waves look pretty mild. Do you think we should take some seasick pills?"

"This from a man who jumps out of planes?"

He shrugged. "What can I say? I've never been on the ocean before. Lots of lakes though."

"If you start to get woozy, just keep your eyes on the horizon and you'll be fine." She looped her arm through the crook of his. "Look, there's a line. We can check out the shops after so let's hurry. I want to get a good spot on the boat so we can see whales or dolphins or maybe even sharks."

He gave a hearty chuckle. "We might not see anything but beautiful coastline, an old lighthouse, and some houses that would make our wallets screech."

The group in line to board was a mixture of couples, young, old, and families. Tric watched a young boy edging closer to the edge of the pier and could hear him trying to convince his mom to go to the amusement rides instead of the boat. The mother was rapidly losing patience and Tric had to wonder why the family wasn't doing something more kid-friendly.

They inched closer to boarding and the family was still in line. This should make for an interesting trip, Tric thought. When it was their turn to board, Kelly wanted to go to the right. The family went to the left, the little boy scuffing his feet as his hand slid along the rail.

Kelly and Tric moved to the front of the boat and took seats overlooking the water. They sat under a canvas shading them from the brilliant sun. She had been right. The waves were rolling gently. He didn't think he'd have any issues with seasickness.

The captain's voice came over the loudspeaker, letting everyone know they were casting off. He relayed a few facts about how far out they were going and what they could expect to see. Once they were away from the dock, a crew member came around to take their drink order.

Tric eased his arm around Kelly's shoulders and she glanced his way. It was too bad he couldn't see her eyes, but her lips tipped up in a smile.

Fifteen minutes after getting underway, the billows of white canvas were full with the steady breeze. The ship skimmed over the open water while members of the crew made the rounds, sharing tidbits of information about the homes they were passing on the shore. Out of the corner of his eye, he saw the young boy who had been getting into mischief on the dock cast a furtive look at his parents. Pulling his attention away from the scenery, he couldn't help but wonder what the kid was up to. Tric continued to keep one eye on the boy while he edged even closer to the rail until he lifted his sneaker-clad foot to the bottom rail. Tric's heartbeat kicked up, and then everything went into slow motion. The boy didn't hesitate. He scrambled up the railing and leaned precariously over the top. Tric dropped his cane and with a few long strides raced across the deck. His training kicking in for action, he didn't call out so as not to startle the boy. He stretched out his arms just as the boy's sneaker-clad foot came in contact with the top of the rail and slipped. Tric grabbed the boy's midsection and hauled him back against his chest with a thud.

An ear-splitting wail reached Tric. It was the boy's mother and as he set the boy down, a man yanked the kid into his arms. Tric took a step back, relieved it was over and the boy was standing on the wood deck.

Kelly was suddenly by Tric's side, asking him if he was okay. He gave her a fast hug but he needed to confirm the boy was unharmed. There would be time to reassure her.

"Ma'am." He touched the mother's arm. "Is your son okay?"

Sobbing, she threw her arms around Tric. "Thank you for saving my baby. I was distracted and I froze when I saw him on the rail. If it hadn't been for you"—she shuddered—"he, he can't swim."

The father's face was ashen as he held his wife and son close. "Thank you."

Tric dropped to one knee on the deck of the boat, and his bad leg protested the angle. "Hey there. Are you alright?"

The boy's chin trembled and tears filled his eyes.

A crew member rushed over. "Is everyone okay?"

It seemed like it had been hours since the kid began to climb but from start to finish it had been less than a minute. Tric looked up. "We're both fine." He turned to the boy. "Will you keep your feet on the deck?"

"I will."

Kelly slipped her chilly hand in his and he rose to his feet, his bad leg groaning in protest. He hadn't thought today was going to involve sprinting across the teak deck, but he was glad he'd been paying attention.

Tric gave the family a brisk nod and let Kelly lead him back to the other side of the boat. She pulled him into a hug and he held her tight against his chest.

"I'm glad you saw him before it became a tragedy, but are you sure about your leg?"

Still quaking inside, he savored the moment, holding Kelly close in his arms as his pulse returned to normal. "I'm fine." But he wanted to hold her a little longer. It felt so right to have her in his arms.

9

*K*elly clung to Tric's hand as her heart fell back into a steady rhythm. All she could picture was the boy tumbling headfirst into the ocean. Her need to be close to Tric was as much for her as it was for him. At this very minute, she wished their feet were on dry land, but there was a long cruise ahead of them.

"Sir, are you okay?" One of the ship's crew members came from the stern and stood in front of them. He held out his hand to shake Tric's hand. "Thank you for your quick action. There is no telling if the ship's undertow would have dragged him under the boat. If that had happened—" The words hung in the air.

"It didn't." Tric's response didn't hold any malice or anger. He sounded like a man whose adrenaline rush had crashed. "Has someone checked on the boy, just to make sure he's really okay?"

"Our medic is checking him over just to be sure. Would you like me to send the medic over? I couldn't help but notice you limping."

"No, thank you."

"May we have a couple bottles of water?" Kelly squeezed his hand as she looked at the crew member.

"Of course, miss." He gestured to one of the roaming crew members. "Please bring this couple anything they need or want with our compliments for the remainder of the cruise."

Another person returned with a couple of bottles of water and handed them to Tric and Kelly.

His hand touched hers. "Any chance you have ibuprofen in there?"

She opened her bag and handed Tric the bottle.

While they sat with their fingers still entwined, she could feel his body begin to relax. They sat watching the horizon slide by with endless ocean in front of them.

Softly, for his ears alone, she said, "You're very brave."

"Anybody would have done the same."

"Apparently, the only person who was paying attention was you. What caught your eye?"

"It was when we were on the pier. He was so fidgety, and his parents were busy enjoying themselves. They didn't realize he needed some attention. It wasn't their fault; it was just one of those things that could happen. Thankfully, I had a clear view of him and just happened to catch the moment he slunk away, and as soon as his foot hit the bottom rail, I was on the move."

"You should have shouted to his parents. They were closer."

"I'm programmed to react and who knows? Shouting might have distracted him and childish curiosity could have become a tragedy."

She gave an involuntary shudder.

He brushed the hair back from her face and cupped her cheek. "But it didn't. The boy's fine and he had a good scare, so he won't be trying something like that anytime soon."

His fingers were warm and her skin tingled under his touch. Looking at his face, she wondered what it would be like to see it every day for longer than the few weeks that were left of his trip. Her breath caught, surprised at how the thought of him leaving cast a shadow over the moment.

He said, "We should focus on the view and have something more to drink than water. Lemonade, maybe?"

She touched his cheek. "I'll get us some."

"*I*'ll come with you." He stood, testing the weight on his leg. So far so good. Using his cane for support, he took a tentative step. His leg trembled a small amount, but it would be okay, even with the boat deck rolling under him.

At the bar, a man clasped his hand and gave it a firm shake. "Man, that was amazing how you reached that kid before he fell over. You're a hero."

Tric felt his cheeks flush and cleared his throat as he glanced at Kelly before looking back at the man. "I was just watching at the right moment. Anyone would have done the same." He preferred to fade into the background and not be singled out.

The man continued with a shake of his head. "Kids. They're like lightning, fast-moving and at times lethal."

He could feel the warmth of Kelly's body as she took a step closer to him at the word *lethal*. "The main thing is he's okay." How many times would he have to say that? Granted, this was only the third person besides Kelly and the boy's parents, but he wanted to enjoy this time with her. After all, they were on a date. Flashing Kelly a smile, he said to the man, "I promised the lady a lemonade, so please excuse us."

The guy pulled out his wallet. "It's on me."

Before Tric could protest, he had paid for the drinks and walked away.

Kelly ordered for them and Tric scanned the deck. People seemed to be holding on to their kids a little tighter than before, but it could be his imagination. His eyes locked with the boy's father. His face was solemn as he placed his hand over his chest and nodded to Tric.

He couldn't begin to understand how that dad might be feeling. He slipped an arm around Kelly's waist. Her nearness was comforting.

As she handed him an insulated to-go cup, she stuck a straw through the lid. "Want to go stand by the rail? Maybe we can see a dolphin or some other kind of fish."

People had stopped pointing at them and thankfully returned to watching the water. Tric took her hand and they walked hand in hand to an open spot. The salty breeze was refreshing, and he put his arm around her shoulders. She smiled as she watched the water, and the serene expression on her face made it obvious she was enjoying herself.

Kelly's voice was filled with excitement. "Look!"

He followed the line her pointing finger made and watched as a dolphin breached the surface, and soon there were several running parallel to the boat.

"I've never seen dolphins in the wild before."

The wonder in her voice matched how he felt. Time seemed to slow as they glided over the water. He was starting to feel at home here, like he had a connection to the ocean and to the woman next to him. Sharing the silence held a promise of what could be. There was no denying he liked her, but it was more than physical attraction, and he wondered what it would feel like to spend more time with her. If he took a leap of faith and left smoke jumping behind, what could he do here? He couldn't make this decision on the basis of a woman alone, no matter how she made his heart race, but thinking of returning to Chicago and his lonely life was soul-crushing.

"Hello? Did I lose you?"

Her voice pulled him back. "If four months ago, while I was lying in a hospital bed with tubes running in and out of me, someone said I'd be standing on a sailboat, I never would have believed them. And now I'm with a beautiful woman, watching dolphins frolic. This is one of the best days of my life."

She bumped her body against his. "The day is young."

He held her close. "So it is."

*A*fter Tric and Kelly disembarked from the boat, they strolled hand in hand around the pier, looking in shop windows but not going inside. It seemed they were happy being together.

He liked the feel of her hand in his, solid and sweet. "It's a little early for dinner. What do you want to do next? The choice is yours."

Kelly sighed as she looked around. "There are so many fun things we could do—play mini golf, ride the Ferris wheel, get a snack, or do them all, and if all else fails, just wander around and people watch."

He gave her a wink. "When was the last time you rode a Ferris wheel?" She tipped her head in his direction and her smile grew.

"Maybe in high school. What about you?"

"The same." He steered her in the direction of the rides. "One trip to the sky is up next." He stopped at a popcorn stand and bought them a bag to share after drenching it in butter and salt. He gave her a side-eye glance. "Don't judge. We can eat healthy tomorrow. It's the weekend."

Once they were belted in, the ride began to move backward and up. It seemed to move at a snail's pace as more riders got on. Finally, they reached the top and slid down the other side.

Kelly squeezed her eyes shut and a nervous laugh escaped her lips. "Wow, this is high. I'll bet it doesn't bother you at all."

"Open your eyes." He brushed his lips across her cheek. "Look. I promise the view is worth the heart pounding, and don't worry. I'm right here."

She didn't look at the view of the ocean but instead looked into his eyes. His heart rate bumped up just like it did before he jumped into a fire. She leaned close and pressed her lips to his, lingering there for a moment. She tasted like melted butter, salt, and sunshine.

"I like this view better."

He put his arm around her shoulders. "Me too." He waited to see if she'd kiss him again, but she snuggled between his body and arm. The car swayed slightly but her body remained loose.

"The ocean is spectacular." Even though she was wearing sunglasses, she shaded her eyes from the sun glinting off the surface of the water. "Do you remember what it was like to jump out of a plane into a fire for the first time?"

"Like so many things in life, there are some moments that you'll always remember." *Like this one.*

"Were you nervous?"

"To be a smoke jumper? There are months of training. Not just for fighting the actual fire, but learning how to jump out of a plane, how to land in the designated zone, and lots of cardio and lifting weights to round out the day. The preparation to be certified is daunting. Think of it like one of the hardest boot camps ever."

"And you willingly put yourself through it for the adrenaline rush?"

The ride went around again and he didn't care if they stayed here forever. "For some people, it might be about the thrill of jumping into a dangerous situation, battling a fire-breathing dragon with an unlimited fuel source. You have no idea how it will react. There are some predictable methods of slaying it and with hard work and luck, we can."

"But for you it's different?"

"After my grandparents came here from Ireland, they fell in love with traveling to all the national parks. Every summer, our family would pack up for two weeks and hit the road, camping in as many parks as we could. That was when I fell in love with the forest. The way all the nooks and crannies of the trees, shrubs, and even the ground was home to so many animals. I came to respect the forest and its life force." He looked out over the ocean as the Ferris wheel began to slow as people got off each time it stopped. "One summer, we went to Alaska and stayed at a camp-ground near Denali."

It was their turn to get off, so he stopped talking. He took her hand and they strolled to the end of the pier.

Kelly said, "You have to finish the story."

He smiled. "Are you impatient to discover my deep secrets?"

"Maybe." The slight Irish lilt in her voice caused his heart to constrict. He could listen to her forever.

"We pitched our tents and off in the distance, there was a column of smoke hovering over one of the mountain ranges. There was a park ranger going around to each campsite, asking us to be extra careful with our fire and to make sure it was out before leaving the site. Oh, and the big thing was to check at the rangers' office before hiking to make sure we stayed out of the path of the wildfire." He remembered that day as clearly as if it were yesterday. "At that time, they were just men who fought those fires, but when I learned there was no way for regular firefighters to get in there and put the blaze out, I was hooked. I wanted to protect the forest."

"The family trip had a profound impact on your future."

"It did, and in a roundabout way, that trip led me to you. But my gran would say it comes down to a little bit of Irish luck."

"Your grandmother sounds just like mine. Everything comes down to luck and I'm glad your family went to Alaska."

"Have you been?" She shook her head, and he said, "You need to put it on your bucket list."

"I just might do that. But until then, how about we hit the mini links and I can dazzle you with my skill at Barnacle Bill's?"

"Another thing I haven't done in years. Lead the way, Miss O'Malley."

---

10

*E*arly evening, after getting trounced by Tric at a quick game of mini golf, they were leaning against the hood of Kelly's car, watching the sun sink toward the horizon. After snacking on popcorn, they weren't in any rush to have dinner; heck, she wasn't in any rush to do much of anything other than be with Tric. This had been the best first date ever—well, except for the kid on the boat.

The sky was changing color from brilliant blue to shades of orange, red, and purple as the sun dipped to the horizon.

"Have you had fun today?"

He caressed her fingers. "I have, and despite all the activity, my leg is achy but better than I thought it would be. Did you change your mind about where you want to have dinner? I couldn't help but notice the food trucks on the wharf. Have you checked them out before?"

"I have, but I really want to show off The Sandbar to you. You'll think you were back home in Chicago at a great pub. It's a traditional Irish pub with a beach flair."

"Sounds like we can't miss it then."

"On St. Paddy's Day, they have the best corned beef dinner. I go there every year with some friends; and remember, you're welcome to join us."

"Thanks, but I might be gone by then."

Her chest tightened a little. She hadn't really thought about him leaving before the end of March but the way she was feeling, she'll have fallen for him hook, line, and sinker if she wasn't careful.

She forced her voice to be bright. "Well, if you're here, you have to come. It's a blast—dancing, food, and of course beer. Lots of Guinness."

With a chuckle, he said, "Sounds like fun." He slid from the hood of the car. "Want to take a stroll before we head back to the wharf?"

A romantic walk on the beach with a handsome man was hard to resist.

*W*hen Kelly brought up St. Patrick's Day, he wanted to say yes to going to the bar, but in good conscience he just couldn't build up either of their hopes.

Holding her hand, he tossed his cane into the car. He wasn't going to need that; he felt amazing.

While they walked over the wave-packed sand, holding hands and just being in the moment, Tric said, "Tell me about the guy who broke your heart."

"It's ancient history." She kicked a small stone in front of her.

"Did he break your heart or just bruise it?" He knew he had his share of breakups but they sucked no matter what side you were on.

She bent over and picked up a bright copper penny from the sand. "Look. It's heads up." She handed it to Tric. "Keep this for good luck."

"Do you believe in luck?"

"Am I Irish?" She took a step and then stopped. "Don't you?"

He reached into his pocket and withdrew a small stone with a hole in the middle. "I carry this with me at all times. I don't know if you've ever seen one but per lore, the stone offers protection from evil and provides luck."

"A *Cloc Costana*." She took it in her hand. It was warm to the touch and seemed to grow warmer the longer she held it. "It's so smooth. Have you had it long?"

"Do you remember when I told you about our family vacation to Alaska?"

She nodded, and then her eyes grew wide. "Did you find it on that trip?"

"I did."

Handing the stone back to him, she said, "It was a sign."

They began to walk. Tric held the stone and the penny.

"He cheated on me with someone I thought was a friend. They got married a few months after we broke up, and last year, I heard they had a couple of kids too."

He gave her hand a squeeze. "I'm so sorry you had to go through that."

"Thanks, but I've moved on. It just took a long time, and then I didn't want to get hurt so I've kept things pretty casual ever since." She gave him a side-look. "I really had fun today. Just being together and getting to know each other is nice."

"Maybe on date two, we can go skydiving if you need more excitement."

She laughed. "I don't need excitement to have fun. I think the best way to get to know someone, and I do mean really know someone, is to keep it simple. There's no reason to be going in tons of directions, doing things and not taking the time to talk. That is the most important part of any relationship—family, friends, or lovers. When it's all said and done, you have to be able to have a conversation with each other."

He couldn't agree more. His steps slowed in sync with Kelly's and they waited while the sun hissed like fire as it touched the water. "Each time I've watched the sun set since I've been here, I can't stop thinking about an old Irish toast. *May the sunbeam from the sunset warm your soul until the sunbeam from the sunrise gladdens your soul.*"

"That's so appropriate."

They waited until the last of the rays slipped beyond the surface of the water.

Kelly tipped her head and a twinkle appeared in her eyes. "What would you say if I suggested we hit the food trucks and take dinner home and kick back on the deck and eat? We can go to the pub another night. And for the record, I'm not cutting our date short, but I would like to eat by candlelight, alone with you."

He took her in his arms and pecked her lips. "Next stop, Fisherman's Wharf food trucks, and then we'll have dinner for two." He slipped his stone and the penny into his pocket. Coming to Last Chance Beach made him think his luck *was* changing. "Kel, why wouldn't the shrimp share?"

Her eyebrow arched and her eyes crinkled. "Because?"

With a hoot, he said, "Because he was shellfish."

• • •

*A*s they drove back to the cottage, Kelly looked at Tric from the corner of her eye. She studied his strong jawline. He had a small scar under his right eye. She itched to reach out and touch it and hear the story about how he got it. Had it happened when he was a kid or on the job fighting a fire?

He glanced at her and gave her a heart-fluttering smile. "What are you thinking about?"

"You're an unexpected interlude."

"That's a first. I've never been referred to as an interlude, and do you mean like the romantic sort or am I a disruption to your life?"

She tapped her chin with her finger. Should she leave him dangling or be honest? Taking the middle of the road, she said, "A little bit of both?"

"I know how you feel. When I came here, I never expected to meet a smart and funny woman." He touched her hand. "And beautiful too."

She could feel the warmth flush her face. She wasn't one of those women whose blush would highlight the cheeks, but instead, her entire face would get deep pink, from her throat to her hairline, and make her faint freckles pop. There was no way to be discreet about a blush.

A slow smile reached his eyes. "You know, one of the things I like most about you is that you wear your emotions on your face. It's honest and refreshing."

She looked out the windshield. "Don't other women you meet lay it on the line?"

"Are you kidding? Some play a weird game of being coy; others put on company manners, and others, well, you don't want to get too close." He pulled in the driveway and turned off the car. Before they got out, he said, "I can see why you stayed here; there is something special about this place, and that includes meeting you. I thought it was funny when my uncle gave me the keychain to the cottage with the shamrock dangling from the ring, but maybe it was a bit of positive change coming my way after a tough few months."

"I'm glad you came. The last few weeks have been fun. Losing my house was the worst thing I've been through and I know it's being rebuilt, but you've added a bit of sparkle to this cottage."

"Let's go inside." He took the bag of food from the back seat and they strolled up the stairs. "I'm curious. Why are all the houses here on stilts that are over a story tall?"

"During hurricane season, if there's flooding, the house won't be damaged and this provides parking or storage. It's all part of the new building codes since Hurricane Andrew."

"That makes sense, and it provides incredible views as a by-product."

She unlocked the door and looked over her shoulder. "I never really thought of that as a perk, but you're right. Even my house is being built on posts and constructed to hurricane codes."

"Do bad storms happen every year? I don't know much about island living."

Moving around the kitchen, Kelly switched on the light over the sink. "We get strong storms at almost any time of year. It has something to do with the cold winds pushing down from the north and colliding with the warm air here. It stirs up the witch of the ocean, and then it's time to take cover."

Together they got dinner plated and uncorked a bottle

of wine and within a few minutes, they were sitting on the deck with candles glowing and the cool evening air wafting around them.

"I'll bet it's thrilling to watch a thunderstorm roll in across the ocean. When I was a kid, my dad and I would sit on the back porch and watch them approach across the lake. I learned to respect the elements but not to be afraid."

"Do you think that's why you've got nerves of steel for smoke jumping?" Kelly poured wine in their glasses.

As they ate, Tric said, "Maybe. I never really thought about it that way. We used to count between the lightning strikes and the thunder to know how close the storm was. My grandparents had a cottage on Lake Geneva, and when my dad was little, the family was up there for a couple of weeks. There was a horrible storm that blew in with lightning and thunder and it had been so hot, they left a couple of windows and doors open for the breeze to change the air inside. Dad was sitting on the sofa playing cards when the lightning struck and bounced into the room. In this case, it was good it had a place to go—out the doorway on the other side." He looked at Kelly with a grin. "The floor was charred from the strike, but Gran always said it was the luck of the Irish that kept the cottage from burning down, and of course St. Brigid's cross over the door. But Dad understood the power of the elements and he taught me and my brothers to be aware but not afraid."

"Smart man."

"One of the best."

"Is the cottage still there?" She wiped tartar sauce from her mouth with a paper napkin.

"It's still in the family and after a few more bedrooms were added, there's room for the entire family to go there every summer. My parents spend most of June through August at the lake and my siblings drift in and out. In the past, I was there in May to open it up for them and then take off for work."

"Maybe you can spend the summer there this year." Instantly she regretted the comment. If he could go to the lake, that meant he hadn't passed his physical and returned to a job he obviously loved. She watched his face fall and she knew she had thrown a wet blanket over their night.

"Maybe." Tric didn't look at her and instead focused on his dinner.

11

*K*elly put a fine point on what could very well be the end of his career. If he was spending the summer at the lake, he wasn't working. He wanted to fool himself into believing life would return to normal, but despite walking and even a light jog today, his leg wasn't as strong as he wanted it to be. The physical was a few weeks away. In his gut, he knew there wasn't enough time.

She placed her hand on his. "I'm sorry."

He gave it a gentle squeeze. "It's all good." He looked out over the ocean. "This would be an awesome place to watch a storm roll in."

"Be careful what you wish for." She laughed. "We don't typically get storms until the temperature really heats up and by that time, you'll be up north."

"What do you normally do on a first date down here?" He tapped his thigh. "I know today wasn't that exciting since I'm a bit slower."

"I'm not exactly a dating pro. I haven't been on a first date in at least five months, and that was a setup from my friend Beth. I wish she was in town so you could meet her, but most of our group rented a house in Colorado from the new year until early March."

"I'm sorry I missed them but it sounds like your date didn't go well."

"The date itself wasn't bad. It was a picnic at the beach with a volleyball game and a bonfire but zero chemistry."

"Well, I'm glad it didn't work out. Otherwise, we wouldn't have gone out today."

With a lift to her chin, she asked, "Tell me. What is your idea of a great first date?"

"Some of that depends on the season. I like going ice skating in winter, maybe geocaching in the spring or fall, and in summer, definitely something on the water."

She nodded and grinned.

"I just described part of our first date with the harbor cruise. If we had been back home, it would have been maybe jet skiing or something a little more adventurous, but I do love the water."

They had finished dinner and he held out his hand. "Care to join me in the glider?"

Once they were sitting shoulder to shoulder, Tric put his arm around her and moved closer so their bodies were touching. As far as he was concerned, this was a very good beginning, but for what? Would she be willing to leave this island and go with him, or was it up to him to change his life? *Whoa, dude. It's been one date. No one is ready to pack up and move anywhere.*

"What's wrong? I felt you stiffen."

"Nothing, I was just thinking about something."

"Anything you want to talk about?"

She turned to look into his eyes and he melted. "No.

It's nothing, and I don't want to waste what is left of our night talking."

He bent his head and his lips brushed hers. A soft sigh escaped and she moved to kiss him in return until she pulled back, breathless.

"You're a good kisser, Patrick."

He tipped his head to the side and caressed her cheek. "It might have had something to do with the kissee."

She leaned against his shoulder and looked out at the water. He turned to look at the way the moon was reflecting in the ripples of the waves.

"Is the tide coming in now?"

"It is. Look at you, aware of the schedule like a local."

"Don't give me too much credit. The waves seem to be louder, that's all."

She paused. "You're out of luck if you thought those were storm waves."

"Can't blame a guy for hoping for a little additional excitement."

"If you're looking for excitement and are back from the mainland, I'm going over to my place tomorrow to check on the progress. You could tag along." She waved a hand. "Never mind. Who wants to look at a bunch of lumber getting hammered together?"

"I'd like to go. I've never been around a house actually being constructed from nothing. Additions, yes, but this could be good information in case I ever want to get into the construction business."

She snorted. "Now you're humoring me."

With a deadpan voice, he said, "It could be my next career."

She sat up. "I hate to call the end of our date, but I have an early phone consultation with a client, and before you ask, yes, on a Sunday, so do you want to walk me to the door?" She wiggled her eyebrows, and he took it as an invitation for another kiss or two.

"I would be happy to accompany you safely to the door." With a halting motion, he pulled her upright and circled his arms around her waist. She was only a few inches shorter than him and he liked it. Walking her backward, he stopped at the threshold.

"Kelly, I had a great time today and tonight. Would you like to go out with me again?"

A little grin sprang across her face. "I think that can be arranged. I'll wait for your call."

He liked how she was playful with her words. "You can count on it, so keep your cell close."

He lowered his mouth to hers. The kiss was slow and long, tasting, exploring, and reveling in the slow burn warming his body. She really was the kind of woman who could make him want a different future.

He said, "Good night, Kelly."

"Sleep well."

She walked into the house and left the door open. He watched until she disappeared down the hallway, and then he went back and sat down. He needed some time to clear his head before he called it a day.

$\mathcal{K}$elly brushed her fingertips over her tingling lips. Kissing Tric hadn't been on her to-do list when she saw him standing in her house, but she was glad she had. He made her pulse race, her knees weak, and the smile that was still on her face—well, this was not her typical first date, but then again, she didn't date people who were staying under her roof, either.

If things were different, she'd want him to stay on the island, but when he talked about his job, it was an integral part of who he was. She was going to enjoy their time together and not worry about a future they couldn't have. How many times in life did you get the chance to date an amazing man? Too often, dating was hard and the guys were so boring, but the first few layers to Tric? Well, she wished she had enough time to peel them away slowly to discover what was at his core.

Kelly was lying in bed with the lights out. She heard the slow shuffle of footsteps coming down the hallway, and they slowed at her door before he continued down the hall. He still had a hitch in his gait at night, but it was better than just a couple of weeks ago. She flipped over a few times while thoughts of him kept her awake—what it would feel like lying in bed with him, curled up close, or waking up next to him, offering him a good morning kiss. Maybe the island would give them both a touch of magic beyond healing his body; maybe both of their hearts would be open to love. Finally, she drifted off with a smile on her lips.

~

The next morning, the sky was filled with large puffy white clouds. Kelly stood on the back deck, watching the sun creep into the sky. She had missed the sunrise but the morning was still spectacular. A sound from the kitchen caused a smile to grace her mouth. Tric was awake.

"Morning," she called over her shoulder, knowing he'd be able to hear her through the open windows.

"Good morning, Kel." He held up the coffee pot. "Do you need a refill?"

"I'm good." She turned her attention back to the water. Being that her uncle's house was at the point of the island, it had a great view of the east, west, and south. All her house had was a view of the western side, but the sunsets would be spectacular from the deck off her bedroom or the great room, once complete.

He joined her on the deck and dropped a small duffel at the top of the stairs. She noticed his coffee was in a to-go cup. He was ready to go to the gym. Would he give her a good morning kiss? Her heart kicked up its beat.

"How did you sleep?" He sipped his coffee. No kiss.

Plastering a smile on her face so he wouldn't see her disappointment, she said, "Great. You?"

"Me too." He took in the view. "Another perfect day in paradise." He took a long sip of the coffee and said, "I was thinking about last night, and dinner from the food truck was great, but do you want to go out tonight? I did promise you a meal in a restaurant."

"Why, are you asking me out on a second date already?"

He gave her a sheepish grin. "I'm smooth, right?"

"Oh very, and dinner tonight sounds great."

"Are you okay with me as your date for Valentine's Day?" He picked up his bag and gave her a slow, sexy smile.

Her heart jumped in her chest; they were having dinner on Valentine's. "I can make a reservation at The Captain's Table if you'd like?"

"Wherever you think would be romantic."

He reached out and caressed her cheek. A pleasurable

shiver raced through her. "I'm already looking forward to it."

"I'm not sure how long I'll be at the gym. It will depend on how I feel." He flexed his biceps. "Getting back in jumping form is arduous work."

She wanted to ask if he was still thinking about going to her house but thought that was asking too much and making them more relationship material. Not like two people just getting to know each other.

He snapped his fingers before he got down the first step. "What time are you going to the house?"

"I was thinking early afternoon, once I know the crew is done with lunch. Why?" She didn't like the indecisive tone to her words.

He grinned at her. "I should be done with my workout by one, if you want company." With a wink, he adjusted his White Sox ballcap.

She let go of the breath that had caught in her chest. "That'll work just fine. But if something comes up or you change your mind, no big deal."

"I'll catch you later." He descended the steps without the cane, another sign that he was getting better.

Her cell phone alarm went off and she went back into the house. It was time to get the day rolling; she had her client phone call and needed to get some website work done too.

Eric pushed through his last set of squats until his injured leg felt like a bowl full of Jell-O. To keep pushing was the only way to get stronger. He walked around the large gym, drinking water while reading various posters on correct posture.

"Hey, how goes the workout?"

The guy who manned the desk was walking in his direction. He stuck out his hand. "I'm Jeremy and I own this place."

"I'm Tric. Good to meet you."

"New to the area?"

"I'm here rehabbing from an injury but thinking I might want to relocate." That wasn't quite the truth but it sounded good.

"Are you staying on the island?"

"Yeah, renting a cottage."

"Great place. I came down from the Big Apple ten years ago on vacation and never went back except to pack my stuff into a van. I've been here ever since." He gestured to Tric's leg. "What happened?"

"Work injury." He was not going to get into how it happened or what he did for work. Best to keep it simple.

"I've noticed you're getting stronger, but make sure you don't push too hard. Sometimes the body can fool us and relapse."

He tipped his bottle. "Thanks. I appreciate that." He drained his water. "I'll see you in a couple of days. Tomorrow is a rest day from weights."

"Might be longer than that. I checked the weather and there's a potential storm brewing in the east. If it follows the projected track, we could be in for some nasty weather. If that happens, no telling if they'll keep the bridge to the island open."

He frowned. "It's good to know but that'll slow down my workouts." Tric draped a towel around his neck and wiped the sweat from his face. "Nice meeting you, Jeremy. I'll catch ya later."

"See ya around and thanks for choosing JM's for your

workout." He went back to the desk and focused his attention on the computer screen.

I wonder if Kelly heard about the storm? I better mention it in case there's something we need to do to get ready. If the bridge does close down, how long is the norm?

He left the parking lot and wondered what people did on an island to prepare for a storm. Well, whatever it was, he'd be right next to Kelly, helping in any way he could.

12

*T*ric made it back from his run in plenty of time to get cleaned up and off to Kelly's construction zone. The morning had sped by, and it was hard to shake the feeling Kelly had forgotten to do something—and then she looked down at her clothes. She was still wearing her pajama pants with a nice top. Video conference calls really were the best. She dashed down the hall to change before Tric came out of the bathroom.

When she returned to the kitchen, he was leaning against the counter dressed in jeans and a purple polo shirt.

"I'm ready before you. Nice." He beamed, and his gaze ran over her outfit. "You look great."

She had put on a skort that matched her top, some earrings, and a touch of makeup so she looked dressy but could still poke around at the jobsite. Then she noticed his cane was leaning against the table. Had he pushed himself too hard at the gym?

"I'm ready to go; I even had time to grab a snack. But

do you need something?" Tric took a banana off the counter and held it out to her. "Fruit?"

"No, I'm all set. I thought we'd get an early dinner. If that's okay with you, I made reservations. We can eat with the silver hair crowd."

He pulled his sunglasses off the top of his head and peered in the mirrored finish. "I didn't turn gray in the shower."

She waved a hand in the air. "Stop. It's just an expression. Besides, that was all I could get, given its Valentine's."

"Then an early dinner it is." He touched her cheek. "See? I'm easy to please."

With a smile, she said, "Yes, you are. Let's get going."

*O*nce they were driving, with Kelly behind the wheel, Tric said, "The owner of the gym was saying something about a possible storm. Have you heard anything?"

"Maybe some rain, but nothing serious. There haven't been any weather alerts on my cell."

"Good." He watched the coastline and took in a lungful of salty air. "If I ever need surgery again, I'm recovering at the beach."

She looked his way before focusing on the road. "Do you know when you're leaving?"

"I think the week before St Patrick's. Just waiting on a couple of things." He didn't elaborate any further.

She gripped the wheel a little tighter. "I hope it all works out the way you want." She slowed and parked in front of what would be her new home. "Look at all those studs."

He laughed. "I assume you mean the framing?"

"Jerk." She jabbed his arm and laughed as he rubbed his arm and pretended that it had hurt. "Come on. I want to take the tour and get a feel for the place. I changed the floor plan."

*W*ith a chuckle, he followed her. He noticed everyone was moving at what he thought was a breakneck pace for a construction zone with saws and fall potential, but what did he know? He definitely wasn't a carpenter.

A gray-haired man dressed in jeans and a polo shirt with the company's logo turned and then approached them with a smile on his face. Tric recognized Mike.

"Kelly. Good to see you again."

"Hi, Mike. You remember Tric? We really wanted to see how things were going." She studied the scene. "It's going up quick."

"All the interior walls will be up by the end of the week, and next we'll get the roof on and button up the exterior. This is a good group of people and they've worked together before."

Tric asked, "Mike, any concern about the storm? A guy at the gym was talking about how it might be a doozy."

He looked up and to the horizon. "It's too early in the season for a major hurricane so I think we'll be okay, and even if there is a little damage, it won't be anything we can't fix quickly."

She gave a nod to Tric and Mike and she seemed satisfied with his response. "Is it okay if we walk through the first floor? I'd like to visualize the space."

"Let me get you both hard hats, and then we can do the

nickel tour." He walked in the direction of his pickup truck.

She flashed Tric a grin with barely contained excitement. "It won't be long before I'm in my own place."

Tric's stomach twisted which took him off guard. He knew their living arrangement was temporary but to have it coming together before his eyes was a reality check.

Mike returned and handed them each a hat. Tric fiddled with the band and put it on and then pointed to hers, which sat at an odd angle.

"Can I fix that for you?"

She handed it over and he adjusted the inner band and passed it back to her. She put it back on her head and struck a pose with a hand on her hip and the other under her chin.

"How do I look?"

He grinned. "Like you're ready to pick up a hammer."

She smiled. "If I thought it would help, I would."

Mike chuckled. "I've got enough people, Kelly, so no need to jump in."

With a smirk, she fell into step next to Mike but held out her hand to Tric. "You're not going to want to miss this."

He liked how their hands fit together like a glove.

"So picture this up one story," Mike said. "You're standing in the entrance from the street-side deck. In front and to the left of you is the great room, with the kitchen to the center and right." He pointed. "The hall will lead to the spare bedroom and in the front, you'll have your office."

She closed her eyes. She could almost see it in her

mind. Big windows. Sunlight filling the house with a warm glow. "What about the third story?"

"That entire space is your master bedroom and bath, with a large deck overlooking the view to the west so you'll have your sunsets."

"Mike, it's going to be the best house on the street."

"Thanks. I felt bad when you lost everything in the fire. We'll have you ready to move in by mid-May."

"Why so long?" She had hoped for April.

Tric gave the palm of her hand a comforting caress and it calmed her.

"We have to wait for cabinetry and other fixtures, but don't worry. If supplies are ahead of schedule, we will be too. I promise we'll get you in as fast as we can so your uncle can start renting out the Shamrock again."

"I know you will, Mike. Thanks for your help."

Tric pulled his hand away and walked to the other side of the space. "How much square footage will you have when it's done?"

Mike rolled back on his heels. "With the decks, garage, and storage, just over three thousand, and lots of windows and sliding doors."

"A perfect island house."

A smile filled his face. "I can picture you here."

"You'll have to come visit me." But would he? That was something to think about another day.

"I might have to." He reached for her hand again like it was the most natural thing to do.

"Alright, Mike, we'll get out of your hair and if something comes up, let me know."

"Actually, if you have time in the next day or so, would you head over to the mainland and stop at the shop to approve the kitchen and bath cabinets and interior doors? I'd like to have Marge get them on order."

She looked at Tric. "Want to go with me?"

He said, "I've got time."

"We can go this afternoon and get it done." She also thought the sooner, the better. "Anything else I should pick out?"

"There's always flooring and bathroom tiles. I can give Marge a heads-up, and she can pull a few things for you to look at."

"Tell her we'll be there in less than a half hour. We have plenty of time before our dinner reservation."

"Will do. Have fun." Mike took their hard hats and walked away.

"We're off to the mainland." She jingled the keys in her hand. "I can drop you at the house if you'd rather hang out here. It'll be kind of boring for you."

"You can tell me more about your life. I know there must be more than just work and walking on the beach and friends who take off for a couple of months." He folded himself into the car.

"Now I'll really bore you to tears." She eased away from the curb and gave him a quick side-glance. "Next stop, the coffee shop. We can't go without being fully caffeinated."

$\mathcal{T}$ric didn't care what Kelly needed to do. Hanging out with her was growing on him. She parked in front of the Playing Hooky Café. "I don't know about you, but I could use an iced coffee."

"With a shot of espresso." He grinned. "I could use an extra jolt of caffeine."

"And a cookie." She held open the door and they entered the shop. The aromas of fresh-brewed coffee and homemade cookies hung in the air. Being with Kelly was easy and he liked how she made something ordinary like grabbing coffee feel special.

Coffee and snacks in hand, Tric waited until they were headed in the direction of the bridge to say, "You never did say what you like to do on dates. Do you like adventure, experiences, or just hanging out?" He bit into a cookie.

"It really doesn't matter what we do, but I guess I enjoy different experiences like the harbor cruise, and I love history, so discovering places like the old lighthouse is cool."

As they approached the bridge, a warning tone came over her cell. She had it in the holder on the dash and glanced at it but while driving, she couldn't read it. "What does that say?"

He took it and read. "There's a storm watch starting tomorrow morning. There could be high winds and heavy rain is expected."

"Hmm, that's interesting. You just might get to experience another fun part of island living."

"But it could avoid us altogether, right?" As odd as it might seem, he was kind of excited to experience the storm.

"All depends on the jet stream. While we're out, we'll pick up a few things like water and batteries since I'm not sure what emergency supplies my uncle has in stock. We'll also need to get some food that won't need to be cooked. I'm not sure what we have left since your appetite reminds me of a teenager." She poked his leg and laughed.

"It's the workouts plus healing. It takes a lot of calories for both."

She gave him a saucy wink and let her gaze roam over his jean-clad legs. "It looks good on you. But we should stock up a bit. There's a gas grill underneath the porch. We could pick up burgers and dogs. There's a protected area where we can safely grill if needed."

"Right." He wiped the cookie crumbs from his finger-tips on his jeans.

They crossed the bridge and merged into heavier traffic on the other side. It was like driving in any small city; the beach feel was lost, as if coming through a portal into another dimension.

She laughed as she navigated the traffic.

"What?" He half turned in his seat.

"I was just thinking leaving the beach is like traveling to a foreign country. I rarely come to the mainland. Every-thing I want or need is on the island."

"Would you ever leave?"

"Before relocating, I was in a small town north of Boston. New England is beautiful, but I can't see myself leaving Last Chance Beach anytime soon."

That answered one question for him. If there was to be a long-term relationship with her, it would have to be here.

She pulled into a large industrial plaza and recon-firmed what she had been thinking; this was a world away from the beach.

She dropped her keys in her bag before getting out of the car. "This shouldn't take long. I know exactly what I want, and then we'll go to a warehouse store, grab supplies, and head for home."

"Will that give us enough time to get to dinner?" He couldn't wait to see her dressed up for the evening.

She gave him a slow, sensual smile. "Plenty."

· · ·

inally, they were on their way back over the bridge, and Kelly could feel her pulse rate slow once she was driving in the direction of the cottage. The back of the car was full of supplies to tide them over for a week, if needed. Whatever they didn't use, she'd save and take to her house for hurricane season. "Thanks for coming with me today. I know it took longer than I planned, but it's good to have it all done. I hope the paint colors work out, but even if they don't, paint is easy to change."

"It was fun." Before he could continue, the warning tones went off on her cell again.

She read the message out loud while stopped at a traffic light. "The storm has been upgraded with winds in excess of fifty miles per hour, rain at the rate of at least one inch per hour, and we can expect power outages and minor flooding. But it's not going to start until tomorrow afternoon." She looked at him, unable to hide her concern. "We'll have to button up the house in the morning. Get the hurricane shutters secured and move the deck furniture into storage. The cottage will get hit hard, as the storm is coming in from the east, and past experience tells me it'll be like a freight train."

"Don't worry. We'll get it taken care of. But if you want, we can do some of it tonight and get a jump on things." He took her hand and didn't let go. "We'll ride out the storm together."

For the first time, she was glad she didn't have to be alone during a storm. "I appreciate that."

• • •

A half hour later, Kelly came out of her room to find Tric standing by the glass doors, looking at the view. Kelly cleared her throat and he turned.

He ran an appreciative look over her. "You look beautiful."

She had taken special care in choosing her outfit. The pale-pink dress had short fluttery sleeves and a V-neckline. It grazed her knees, and she wore silver high-heeled sandals. By the look on Tric's face, she knew she had chosen the right dress for their date. She gave him a wide smile. "You're looking pretty handsome too." He had on a creamy-yellow button-down shirt, a floral tie, dark slacks, and black tie shoes. Did he bring the dressy clothes with him to the beach? She was curious but it didn't matter. Either way, he caused her mouth to go dry and he was just the tall drink of water she needed to quench her thirst.

A smile quirked the corners of his mouth. "Now, about dinner."

He held out his hand and she took it. "I need to warn you, it might be a little romantic, with candles and music playing."

"I'm counting on it." He kissed her cheek and she breathed in his spicy cologne. "There isn't a better way for us to spend the evening."

T ric and Kelly lingered over dessert and coffee. He wasn't in any rush to get home. He gestured to the dance floor and the older couples, each in their own bubbles, dancing like they didn't have a care in the world other than being in each other's arms.

He held out his hand. "Dance with me?"

"I'd like that." She glanced at his leg, and he shook his head.

"No fancy footwork tonight, but the next time."

She rose from her chair, her hand in his, and he guided her to the polished wood floor where he twirled her into his chest and slipped his right arm around her waist, interlacing their fingers. Holding her close, they danced cheek to cheek. He couldn't stop himself; he was falling in love with this woman.

He looked into her eyes. "Are you enjoying yourself?"

Her mouth begged to be kissed but he needed to know if she was happy.

She looked deep into his eyes, and she whispered, "The best night of my life."

"Mine too." He lowered his mouth to hers, slowly kissing her. The night didn't need to ever end.

13

The next morning Tric's adrenaline was pumping similar to preparing to head into an inferno as he watched the fiery sunrise. At least this time he didn't need to jump out of a plane to get into the thick of things. He wasn't sure if Kelly was awake so he carried his sneakers as he walked softly down the hall and started a large pot of coffee. He was making extra so they could freeze some for iced coffee later.

They had watched the weather last night after they got home from dinner. The storm was still due in the early afternoon so they had time to secure the cottage.

He set two mugs on the counter when he heard footsteps on the outside stairs. He looked out the kitchen window and opened the door. His brow lifted. "What are you doing out here?"

"I couldn't sleep, so I got started on the smaller items. So far, the grill's been secured and the beach chairs." She sniffed the air. "Is that coffee?"

"Yes. Let's have breakfast, and then we can plow through the to-do list." He glanced in the direction of the sliding doors. Plenty of wispy clouds were streaked across the blue sky. "Think we could walk down to the beach and watch the storm roll in?"

She laughed. "Still looking for the thrill?"

He shrugged like it wasn't any big deal, but he did want to witness the intensity of the storm. "What can I say? It's my dad's fault."

"Remind me to have a talk with your dad, but for right now, promise me if you're ever faced with a hurricane, you won't want to hang out on the beach."

"Only until the wind knocks me over." He handed her a full mug of coffee and added a splash of cream to it.

"Thanks, but you don't need to fix breakfast."

"We'll do it together."

They scrambled up a few eggs and sausage along with toast. Who knew if they'd be able to have a hot meal later. They might be eating sandwiches.

"Can you show me the storage space after we eat? Then we can figure out how to get everything in there."

She shook her head. "I don't know if there's enough space. We may need to put some stuff in the living room." Her face lit up. "Actually, we could do that with the chaise lounge chairs and the glider and just move the rest into the storage room. It'll be easier getting them in here than down the stairs."

"It's no problem to get them down there. The stairs are wide enough." He gave her an assessing look. "Are you wondering if my leg can handle the task?"

She scooped eggs into her mouth and wouldn't look him directly in the eye. "Carrying furniture is hard work."

"Kelly, I'm fine. I appreciate that you're concerned but it's like this place has magic. My leg is stronger than I thought possible in a few short weeks."

"I've been telling you there is something about the island. She gave a slow shake of her head. "However, I am not going to take the chance you injure your leg and that's the reason you don't pass the readiness test. It's too important. We can put the stuff in the house."

Her cell rang. "I have to get this." She got up and looked at the caller ID. "Hey, Uncle Kevin." She pushed her empty plate to the center of the table. "We're ready."

Tric picked up the plates and put them in the sink.

She was nodding. "That's right. Tric and I are moving all the furniture in and the hurricane shutters will be secured last. What?" She looked at Tric and continued. "I didn't know you had a generator on order. I haven't gotten a call for install."

She nodded. "Please don't worry. We've got this covered. In fact, Tric's looking forward to the storm." She laughed. "I know. They're not like landlocked storms." She grew serious. "Okay, I'll call when it's over and if we lose power, don't worry. We loaded up on supplies."

After she said goodbye, she pushed back from the table. "I need to charge my power bank so we'll have cell phones."

"I've got one too. I'll do the same."

After talking to her uncle, she seemed more on edge. As she walked by him, he touched her arm. "Are you alright?"

"Sure."

He wasn't convinced but made short work of cleaning the kitchen and then got his power bank plugged into the power strip in the kitchen, and as an afterthought, he put his phone on the charger too.

He was going to check on Kelly when she emerged from her office.

"I had to take care of my computers, do backups, and power everything down just to be safe." She smiled at his phone and power bank charging and followed suit. "We should get the back side done since those chairs stack, and Uncle Kevin said to rearrange the storage space and figure out what else will fit."

Nothing more was implied about him not being able to handle it. They worked for the next few hours with an easy companionship. She didn't mention what her uncle had said to upset her.

"Is there anything you want to talk about?"

She flashed him a look. He could see her eyes were filled with worry.

"Uncle Kevin said if the winds get as bad as predicted, it could destroy the framing at my house. That would mean a huge delay for moving out of here."

"Has he rented the place, giving you a deadline?" He didn't want to think a family member could be that unfeeling, but he knew not everyone was like his family. They'd do anything for anyone.

She shook her head. "No, nothing like that, but I know how much weekly rentals go for around here, and I'm sure my rent covers very little of the monthly expenses. I've offered more, but he says family comes first."

He breathed an internal sigh of relief. "He sounds like he's got your best interests at heart."

"He's a good guy and he's my godfather, so I think that adds to the bond." Her voice dropped. "After my dad passed away, Uncle Kevin, who's my father's brother, stepped in to be more like a dad."

"Did he live near the rest of the family when you were growing up?"

"The same neighborhood. You know how some families are, thicker than cold oatmeal at the bottom of the pot." She laughed as he furrowed his brow. "What? You don't like oatmeal?"

"Not with that description." He chuckled as they continued to work and talk. After putting the last of the furniture in the living room because there was no room left in the storage space, he said, "That's the last of it. Lunch on the beach with the waves whipping up would be fun."

"You have an interesting idea of fun, but we just need to unhook the glider from the roof rafters, and then that's it."

He clapped his hands together. "Let's put a hustle in your bustle." He paused to look out at the water. "Whoa. Do you see those clouds? How fast do you think they're moving?"

"I have no idea, but past experience would indicate it's going to be a helluva storm. When we come up from lunch, we'll have to secure the last of the shutters over the sliders, and then we'll be set."

"How will we watch the storm?"

Her mouth gaped open. "You're serious?"

He grinned as she reached up and unclipped one side of the glider. Kelly held one end steady and waited for him to unclip the other side. He then picked up one end. "Ready?"

They eased it through the open door and found a place to set it.

"Now we can go to the beach." Kelly gave him a grin. "I'm going to wash up first."

"I'll throw together some sandwiches."

She brushed against him as she squeezed past all the extra furniture and his pulse jackhammered. The air between them sizzled like lightning had struck inside the house. Her eyes widened and her pupils got bigger as she recognized it too. She tore her gaze away.

"I'll be right back."

*T*ric held Kelly's hand as they crossed the street to the deserted beach, save for a couple of people surfing.

"I've wanted to tell you all morning, but last night was amazing."

She looked at him from the corner of her eye. "Are you saying that after all the mundane things we did, dinner was the highlight of your day?"

He stopped walking and pulled her to his chest while she laughed. "Not exactly, and you know it. I loved every moment spent with you, but the highlight was dancing with you, and then that goodnight kiss seemed to hold a hint of promise for maybe something more?"

She looked away and he wondered if he had read too much into the kiss.

"It's complicated."

He relaxed his arms and she took a step back. "You're leaving, and as much as I like you, I don't want either of us to get hurt when the next few weeks are history. Casual dating and a few kisses are all I can handle. I'm not a casual relationship kind of a girl."

He understood and respected her for being honest. Breaking eye contact, he said, "Kel, it's okay. I get it." He didn't have to like it though. He wanted them to be very close, so close he could hear the beating of her heart.

He decided to make this easier on both of them so he pointed to people in the water. "I've seen this on The Weather Channel when they're covering hurricanes.

What is it with surfers playing chicken with the elements?"

"I don't know if it's the lure of high waves or that they have the ocean to themselves, but we have a few locals who are out here as often as possible, no matter the time of year or weather. They'll only come in when the lightning starts."

"Well, at least they have some sense."

The air was now bringing a chill and the wind was growing in strength. Heavy dark clouds had covered what was left of the bright-blue sky.

Once they stepped on the beach, she tugged him closer to a spot between the water and the road. She flicked out the blanket she had brought, fighting the wind to get it in place.

"We might not have a lot of time before it starts to rain."

He sank into the chilly sand and leaned back on his hands with his legs stretched out in front of him. "For a cool factor, this is it. Other than meeting you, this will be the highlight of my trip."

"You're easy to please."

He handed her a sandwich from the bag he had carried. "Peanut butter and jelly?"

"*T*he perfect beach lunch." She scooched closer to Tric to watch the water. His nearness was calming and thrilling at the same time. She had felt another jolt of electricity between them when they were at the house and now it simmered under the surface. She looked his way and he leaned into her.

"What are you thinking?"

"This is the first time I've sat on the beach and waited for a storm. It seems a little crazy when we could be sitting on the deck with easy access to a safe haven."

"The first rumble of thunder—or even a single rain-drop—we'll be on our way back across the street." His finger trailed down her cheek and tilted her face up. His lips hovered over hers and her eyes widened, then she quickly closed them as he lowered his mouth and kissed her tenderly. "You don't have to worry. I'll protect you."

But who was going to protect her heart? Despite what they had talked about a few minutes ago, she wanted to be closer to him.

Before she threw herself against his chest, throwing all caution to the wind, she said, "Do you like games?"

He blinked hard. "Huh? Games?"

"You know Scrabble, Monopoly, cards?"

"Oh, you mean like if we lose power and we can't binge-watch something on Netflix? Those kinds of games?"

She cleared her throat so as not to stammer. "Exactly. I'm more of a Scrabble girl and wondered what your pref-erence was."

"I like pretty much anything but I'm not very good. I haven't played board games in years."

The surfers caught a huge wave and off in the distance, the first glow of lightning flashed.

"How many miles out do you think that is?"

"Not as far as you think." Kelly tipped her head back, her face to the sky, and waited for the first drop. It was only moments away.

And then the clouds let loose, and it wasn't a nice drop or two but a downpour.

Shrieking, she leaped up and pulled Tric to his feet. Laughing, she said, "Come on."

He flicked the blanket and tucked it under his arm, and she grabbed the tote bag that held the last of their lunch. With hands clasped, they ran like kids, splashing through the puddles in the street and up the stairs to the cottage. Drenched, they stood with their backs against the kitchen door, panting from their mad dash. She flashed him a teasing grin. "Look at you run!"

He flexed his leg and grinned. "It doesn't even twinge."

She gave him a playful poke on his arm. "It's island magic." Another loud crack of thunder and she jumped. "And now it really begins."

14

The wind howled like a banshee around the cottage with a ferocity that Tric had never experienced before—except for a wildfire, which was like the rumble of a jet plane. He glanced at Kelly standing in the middle of the room, twirling the end of her dripping ponytail as she looked toward the side window. They had wanted to leave one clear to monitor the storm, but it looked like she was having second thoughts. He was reminded of *The Wizard of Oz* movie with debris dancing past the window.

"Are you doing okay?"

"Yeah. I'm just wondering if we should have covered that window too. But it's too late."

"I can secure it if you want." The hurricane shutters looked decorative, but they folded over the glass and were secured in place with bolts and clips. It would be challenging to do the right side, but the left would be forced closed as soon as he freed it from the open position. The bigger concern was if the force of it slamming would cause the window to shatter.

She looked outside and gave him a tight smile. "No. It's not safe to be out there. If the window breaks, we can get it fixed, and we're here so we can take care of protecting the inside of the house."

"I get it. This is your uncle's place and you don't want anything to happen to it. We did all the right things. Look on the positive side; if there was another renter in here, they might not have done all that we did."

"Oh, I know." She shook her arms out and gave him a more relaxed smile. "I'm a worry wart."

His hand flew to his mouth and he pretended to be surprised. "I had no idea."

"Stop. Now, movies or game time?"

"Movie, and ladies' choice." He dropped on the couch and patted the cushion next to him. "Have a seat."

A *thud* resounded from the front side of the house. It was near one of the bedrooms. He got up and they hurried down the hall to check it out. There was no way to tell what had hit the house, but he wanted to make sure the shutters had held.

Kelly looked down. "You're not using your cane?"

He flexed his leg at the knee. "It feels pretty good. Must be the sea air." Some of this had to do with the exercise regimen his physical therapist had sent with him. Another component was that he was happy and he had become a believer about the island magic.

"Ready for a movie? I was thinking *Armageddon* or *Twister* or some other disaster kind of flick. It'd be fitting, considering the weather we're having."

"As long as we're not faced with the end of the world due to some giant meteor." He liked that spending time with her was easy. He had reined in some of his practical jokester ways since he wasn't sure how she'd take them, but holding back wasn't showing his true colors. He needed to just be who he was and hopefully she'd still like him hanging around.

She turned on the television and scrolled through Netflix before finally selecting a movie. The opening credits rolled, and he put his arm around her shoulders. She picked up her glass of water and just as she tipped it up, he tapped her elbow so water sloshed out and dribbled down her chin.

Laughing, she wiped her face dry. "You know about payback?"

He kissed her cheek. "I'll look forward to you trying to prank me, but others have tried and failed."

She gave him a sly grin. "Don't underestimate me. I've been known to have a funny bone on occasion."

*T*he end credits rolled, and remnants of snacks sat forgotten on the coffee table while the storm continued to roar, but with less intensity. The television flickered once, and then the screen went dark. They sat in the shadows for a few minutes. Kelly was wondering if the power would come back on immediately, but after what seemed like a mini eternity, she said, "Well, time for the backup plan."

"How long could the power be out?"

"It can vary, but with the storm finally letting up, I'm guessing it will be several hours, or maybe by morning at the latest."

She went into the kitchen and set out the battery-operated candles. Tric jumped in and once they were scattered around the room, he asked her what they needed to do next.

The candlelight made the room feel small and romantic and she could picture them snuggled on the couch. However, she needed to stay focused and keep their relationship more casual.

"Scrabble?" Her voice cracked.

"Are you going to spot me points?"

"You're joking." She gave him her best stink eye.

"Can I use a dictionary?"

This time, she just laughed. "The games are in the cabinet next to the slider. I'll meet you at the table."

Putting space between the two of them was a smart idea. She placed a few more candles on the table but when she turned, she ran into him. He put his arms around her waist and she melted into them.

She tipped her head back. "Kiss me. I'm Irish."

He lowered his mouth, brushing over her lips.

Throwing caution to the wind, she kissed him from the depths of her soul. She wanted to be close to him, closer than she had been to anyone since her ex. Time became meaningless as they enjoyed being in each other's arms. Tric pulled away and cupped her cheek in his hand.

"Kelly, we should slow things down."

She took a step back and tumbled into a chair. Running a hand over her hair, she wouldn't look him in the eye. The longing in his mirrored how she felt but she chalked it up to the circumstances and not anything more serious. *He's leaving. Don't start something that will hurt you in the end.*

Flipping open the box top, she pulled out the game board and set everything up. She could feel Tric watching her.

"Kelly."

She could hear the unasked question in his voice. "Tric,

I'm sorry for the mixed messages. I got caught up in the moment and I do like you, but you're going back to your old life soon."

"I like you too. Do you want me to leave tomorrow so we can avoid any complications? I can head back to Chicago."

Even though it was going to hurt when he left, she wanted to spend all the time she could with him. Meeting him gave her hope there was a nice man out there for her, and it showed her it was time to start dating, even if it wouldn't be him.

"No, I want you to stay, but I think we need to be more like good friends. Platonic friends."

"I can be a good friend, without the kissing."

She was going to miss the kissing and where it might have led. "Good." She stuck out her hand. "Roomies?"

"I think we've been here before."

"You can never have too many friends."

He dipped his head. "Especially one as pretty as you."

*S*he had just fractured his heart. He hoped there might be more between them, but he wasn't stupid. She was trying to protect herself. He'd settle for friendship, but there was something about this woman. It was so easy between them, like they had known each other for a long time, but it was exciting to discover things about her and how well they meshed. He needed to keep things easy and comfortable for them both.

Sitting in the chair across from her, he said, "Are you ready to pick a tile to see who goes first?"

She cocked a brow. "I thought you said you hadn't played in a while?"

He gave her a nonchalant shrug. "When I was in the hospital and laid up, I had to do something while recovering, and some of the guys from my crew came by to keep me company. There are just so many times we could rehash a ball game."

She picked up a tile. It was a *B*. "Your turn."

He watched her as he selected a tile. "Blank."

"You're one lucky guy." She mixed up the tiles and put them back and they each selected starting letters.

Tric smothered a laugh. Looking at his tiles, he had a high scoring word.

She rolled her eyes. "What now?"

He set them out and spelled *QUICK*.

"Are you kidding me? Twenty points?" She tapped her fingers on the tabletop. A slow smile spread over her face. "The game is young, but here you go. *AQUA*. Thirteen points."

She was competitive. This was going to be a lot more fun than he had expected, and infinitely better than hanging with the guys.

"Game on, O'Malley."

She danced in her seat. "What's a good board game for doctors?"

"Scrabble?"

She shook her head. "Nope. Scribble."

He gave a chuckle. "Darlin'," he drawled, "I think we both can skip open mic night at the bar."

"Speak for yourself. I'm just warming up my comedy routine." She pointed to the board. "Your turn."

He studied his tiles and then put out two. *RUN*. "I might have gotten a little cocky."

She leaned across the table and patted his hand. "It happens, but we have a long way to go. Don't lose hope yet." The television flicked and the refrigerator began to hum.

"Power's back." He pushed back his chair.

"Sit. We're not leaving until the game's over."

He gave her a mock salute. "Yes, ma'am."

A satisfied grin flashed across her face. "Now, where were we?"

15

The next morning, Kelly checked the weather app on her phone. It promised full sun and clear skies for the next week. The first step after a quick breakfast was securing the hurricane shutters open—she needed lots of sun—and then getting all the furniture back in place, as long as there wasn't any damage. Her thoughts drifted to her house. As soon as she walked around here, she needed to get across the island. Hopefully it wasn't too bad.

She rolled over and listened to see if she could hear Tric moving about. How quickly she had become accustomed to having him here. Life would be so quiet when he left. No, it would be empty.

A soft *thud* drifted to her ears. He was up. She flicked back the covers and changed clothes. With a quick stop to brush her teeth and hair, she was ready to start her day.

"Good morning," she chirped as she glanced into the living area. Where was the deck furniture? "What time did you get up?"

"An hour or so ago. I couldn't sleep and thought you'd

like to get over to your house as soon as possible. So I put things back in place. I'll need your help putting the glider back up."

She crossed her arms across her chest. "You should have woken me up. I would have helped."

"I look at it as exercise." He handed her a mug of coffee. "For you."

"Thank you. You've spoiled me by making coffee every morning."

"It's nothing." He looked at her over his mug. "Do you want company when you check on your place?"

"If you have time." She'd like the company. Facing another disaster alone would be hard.

"My day is free since the bridge is closed. Something about a boat breaking loose from the marina."

"Maybe we'll cruise by and check it out later."

They made short work of the glider and grabbed a couple of protein bars for the ride over to her place.

*A*s they drove around the island, the amount of damage to homes and businesses made Kelly's heart sink lower and lower. Roofs were gone, trees and shrubs uprooted, screen porches missing sections, and even a few doors hanging limp on a single hinge. She didn't have a good feeling about what she was going to find.

Tric slowed his car as they approached her driveway and he parked next to the curb. Several pickup trucks had already arrived—Mike's crew, she hoped—and blocked her view. Her throat constricted and dread settled in her stomach as she got out of the car and the building site came into view. She was stunned by the level of destruction. Some of the studs were in splinters; some were leaning precariously inward or laid in the mud. Mike saw them and strode across the muddy ground.

"Kelly, before you say anything, please don't worry. We'll get the site cleaned up by tomorrow and we'll rebuild. But we have a few more construction sites to check on before we can start."

Her heart was in her toes. "This is, well, I'm not even sure what to say. I never expected to feel this bad. It's like the fire all over again."

"I take full responsibility. I should have had the guys sheathe the sides, which would have given the structure more stability."

"If the house can't withstand a thunderstorm, how will it ever take the brunt of a hurricane?" She felt sick to her stomach. All that money literally gone with the wind. "I have to call my insurance company to see what they'll cover."

"I put together a rough draft of what we lost." He took his hard hat off and ran a hand through his short gray hair. "It would have been worse if we had gotten the roof rafters up. That would have set us back a couple of weeks."

"I guess." Despite what Mike said, it had taken a couple of weeks to get this far. They were good but not fast. "How many weeks will this set us back?"

Tric stood by her side like a silent sentry, his presence comforting.

"I intend to bring the house in on time." Mike was doing his best to reassure her. But she still had that lead weight inside.

Tric looked around. "What if I cleaned up the site?

Would it help to get you back on schedule? I can also lend a hand with framing if someone tells me what to do."

She placed her hand on his arm. "Tric, that's a very generous offer, but I can't afford to take on any additional help, especially someone who is untrained."

He waved his hand. "You've misunderstood me. I want to help, Kel. I won't take your money."

"I can't let you do that," she began. "You might strain your leg."

"You need to stop worrying that I'm going to hurt myself. Trust me; I know my limits. If nothing else, I can carry studs and clean up debris. Besides, since I can't get to the gym, this will make a nice substitute." He looked at Mike. "Tell me exactly what you need done and when you come back tomorrow, this place will be in better shape."

He looked from Kelly to Tric. "This is highly unusual. Are you sure you want to spend today working?"

She slid her hand down Tric's arm and squeezed his hand. "We'll work together. Tell us what we need to do and if I have any questions, I'll give you a call."

"As the homeowner, you certainly have the right to clean things up, and if I just happen to have left hard hats and gloves behind, well, you could use them. Oh, and you'll need a few tools. Then take everything that is damaged and dump it in the green dumpster. If something can't be recycled, put it in the red one." He waved for them to follow him. After he handed them hats and gloves, he reminded them to wear both at all times. "Safety first."

Since the first moment they had arrived, she felt hope bubbling up that she'd still be on track to move in.

"I can leave someone to help." Mike looked between them.

Tric said, "Just show us what to leave alone and we'll be good."

She nodded. "We've got this."

They watched as the crew drove off. Kelly slapped the gloves in the palm of her hand. She was bowled over that Tric wanted to help. "This is very generous of you."

He shrugged. "Kind of two sides of the same housing coin. You helped me when you didn't have to, so I'm returning the favor."

Humbled, she stuck the hat on her head. "If you play your cards right, lunch will be on me."

They worked steadily for the next three hours until Kelly flopped down on a stack of new lumber that had already been delivered. Mike wasn't wasting any time in getting back on track.

"Are you hungry?" Kelly asked.

"I thought you'd never say something. I could eat and drink; I'm parched. You're a tough taskmaster."

Her mouth gaped open. "I've been waiting for you to speak up. I didn't want you to think I was lazy or, worse, a wimp."

He rocked back on his heels. "You're saying you haven't taken a break because you didn't want me to think you couldn't keep up?" He chuckled and pulled up the bottom of his tee and wiped his face.

The simple gesture made her mouth go dry as she caught a glimpse of his six-pack abs.

"You'll love this," he said. "I haven't taken a break so you wouldn't think I wasn't recovered."

She pulled out her phone. "In that case, I'm calling the

sandwich shop and asking for delivery. What do you want?"

"Besides a couple bottles of water? Turkey on whole wheat with everything and something sweet—a cookie, brownie, or whatever."

She placed an order for two of everything and in addition to bottled water, she ordered lemonade since she knew he had a weakness for it. The shop made it fresh and it was just sweet enough.

"Lunch will be here in a half hour."

He looked around the yard. "We're almost done. I'll just finish cleaning up that one pile of wood."

"This jobsite will be the tidiest on the island." She took in the immaculate piles of lumber and supplies. The ground had even been raked. Tric had worked hard. It was a glimpse into the smoke jumper and the care that had to be drilled into him for his job.

As Tric finished the final touches on the cleanup, a delivery van pulled in with their lunch. She set it up on the wood she had been using as a bench.

"If you don't come now, I'm eating your sandwich and mine." She stuck straws in cups of lemonade and handed him one as soon as he was within arm's reach.

He took a long drink. "Now that hits the spot."

The makeshift picnic table was covered with paper napkins, sandwiches, and a big bag of potato chips. Having lunch here was better than the deck at Shamrock Cottage and it was something she would remember for a long time.

He looked through the bags. "No pickles?"

Kelly held up a foil-wrapped package that looked like a hot dog. "Got those too."

He leaned in as if he was about to kiss her and then pointed to a spot over her shoulder.

"You should add the barbeque grill right there."

She followed his gesture. "That might be a good spot." She was disappointed; she wanted him to kiss her again. It hadn't even been twenty-four hours since they had agreed to a platonic relationship and she was already missing that part of their budding relationship.

"Good." He polished off his sandwich without further conversation.

She hated the new silence between them. It felt like turning things platonic had also destroyed their ability to simply chat. "Have you thought about what will happen if you don't ace the endurance test?"

He knitted his brows together and paused. "What makes you think I won't?"

"Nothing, but I'm a firm believer in having a backup plan."

He drank from a bottle of water and didn't look at her.

"I'm sorry. I'm out of line."

The silence wrapped around them like a down comforter in summer. Tric toyed with the bottle of water before he finished drinking it.

"I've been thinking about what will happen if I fail. But in my life, failure has never been an option. I'm not sure I know how to start over."

He looked at the ground, but she knew what he had shared was a huge weight he carried.

"Talk to me. Maybe I can help." Her voice was soft.

He lifted his eyes to look at her. "All I've ever done is fight fires and stay in shape to fight them. Yeah, in the off-months, I've worked on forest management, but it's not something I want to do full-time. I'm trained as an EMT but I never took the state exam and I'm not sure if I would want to do that either, but it's an option."

"What about being a teacher or something where you get summers off? I always thought that was a good idea."

"I couldn't see myself in a classroom with a bunch of kids. I like them, but not twenty-five at one time." He shook his head. "I'm coming up empty."

She touched his arm, hoping to offer encouragement and support. "You don't have to decide anything today."

His cell phone rang. "This is it." He looked at Kelly and got up. "Patrick Ryan."

Kelly watched as his face ran through a range of emotions.

"Thank you for calling, and I'll see you in a few days."

"When do you have to leave?" Her heart sank to her toes.

"In ten days." He opened his arms and she jumped into them.

"I'm going to miss you."

He buried his face in her neck. "I'll miss you too."

16

---

*T*he next day, since the bridge was open, Tric went to the gym. It hadn't taken long for the boat to be cleared from underneath it. He needed to have some space from Kelly, not because he didn't want to be with her but because his heart already ached. What would it be like in two weeks when he was a couple thousand miles away?

Her questions had struck a nerve. He had always thought he would have time to decide when he was leaving the crew, but even if he was cleared, would he want to continue now that he saw the chance for a different life, one he hadn't realized he wanted until he met her?

Tric did biceps curls and moved to squats. His leg didn't tremble as much as it had, but by the end of the three sets, there was definite fatigue setting in. He pushed through and moved back to upper body work. He was going to be as fit as possible once he got to Chicago if it killed him in the process.

The gym was pretty empty for a Thursday, but Tric liked it that way. He needed to focus. To think.

Setting the free weights aside, he dropped to the bench and hung his head. What if he took the next phase of his life in a slightly different direction? He could check into joining the EMS squad on the island. He'd have to take a refresher course and then a test, but it was possible. But maybe Kelly wouldn't want him to stay. After all, she was the one who wanted to cool things off the other night despite the sparks that were flying in the middle of a storm.

Since his head wasn't in the gym and that could lead to an injury, he decided to call it a day. He could use some unbiased advice. All he was doing was making his head spin. He packed up and held up a hand to a new guy at the desk before leaving. Sitting in his car, he dialed his mom.

"Hi, Tric. It's good to hear your voice."

Her smile came through the phone. "Same here. Do you have a minute?"

"I have all the time in the world for you. What's up?"

He laid out everything that had happened since coming to Last Chance Beach and meeting Kelly.

"She sounds like a terrific girl. How does she feel about you going back to jumping?"

"We haven't really talked about that specifically. But she asked me what my plan was if I couldn't go back."

"And what was your answer?"

He could hear the unasked question in her voice. Was he going to stay at the beach or return home?

"In my mind, I always thought I'd go back. It never even hit my radar to have a different career path. You know I love what I do, and I always thought I had time to decide when I'd leave. There are people jumping well into their fifties. It's rare, but it does happen."

"But do they have for a personal life?"

He stopped to think of some of the regular crew guys who had worked with him for years. Most didn't have kids and wives. Girlfriends, yes, but like him, after a few years, the relationship was over about the time June rolled around again. He understood it had to be difficult to be part of a couple for only seven months out of the year. Texts or the occasional phone call didn't fill that void.

"No, they don't."

"Son, do you want to have a family of your own? And it's okay if you don't. I'm not asking you to put pressure on you, but that is something you need to consider. All your dad and I want is for you to live a happy life on your own terms."

"I'll be home in a couple of weeks. Maybe I can stop by for dinner on the weekend when I get back? You know, catch up, talk about opening the cottage and stuff."

"The door is always open. Should we make it a family affair and invite everyone?"

With a grin, he said, "How about our first meal is just the four of us—you,, Dad, me, and of course Gran. Then you can plan the welcome home bash."

"Any chance you'll bring Kelly with you?"

"Mom"—that word held a good-natured warning tone —"stop pushing."

"Can't blame your mom for trying."

"I'll see you soon. Love ya."

"I love you, son, and be careful driving."

"Will do." He chuckled as he disconnected. It wouldn't matter how old he got, she'd always tell him to be careful.

He looked around and wondered what he'd do for the

rest of the day. He was at loose ends and a run was possible, but then he'd need a shower, which meant going back to the cottage.

He started his car and headed in the direction of the bridge, and that's when it hit him. He could go work on her house—well, that's if Mike could use some free labor.

*K*elly sat in front of her computer, staring at but not seeing the screen. The memory of holding Tric close the moment she learned he was really leaving would linger forever. Denial had been a nice place to visit and it had felt like she had found the place she had been searching for since coming to Last Chance Beach, but now he was leaving, and probably for good.

There was a catch in her breath and unshed tears. She was going to make what was left of his time here fun. They still needed to get to the lighthouse again and maybe tonight would be a good night to picnic. She shot him a text to see if he was up for one.

Disappointed he didn't respond right away, she refocused her attention on the coding problem in front of her. She reminded herself it was foolish to think he was sitting on his phone, waiting for her text.

After working for another hour, she got up and wandered around the cottage. An incoming text pinged.

Lighthouse sounds great. Be home in a while. Need anything?

Nope, all set. See you later.

She opened the sliders to let the salty air drift through the rooms. Before she went back to work, she tossed together some bruschetta to marinate and skimmed the refrigerator for what else they could take. It looked like a

LUCINDA RACE

good night for antipasto. Humming, she went back to work and willed the rest of the afternoon to fly by.

Several hours later, she heard Tric's footsteps on the stairs. Her heartbeat quickened and she ran a hand over her hair to smooth out any frizz. She looked at her work clothes—yoga pants and an ancient Van Halen t-shirt—and inwardly groaned. She should have changed. Oh, well.

"Hey." He poked his head into her office sporting a wide grin. "Guess where I just came from?"

"The gym?" She was confused. That's where he had planned on going, but he had a faint shine of sweat mixed with sawdust on his face. She narrowed her eyes. "Did you work out?"

"Yeah, I did a short session and then got tired of being inside so I came back over the bridge and found myself at your house—well, what will be your home—and volunteered to help Mike's crew out. Not that they let me use power tools or a hammer. But I'm a quick study and I spent the last hour doing more than just lending muscle."

"You shouldn't be spending your last days working on my house. Hang out on the beach, explore, relax, and have fun. When you get home, it'll still be cold, snowy, and, well, winter." She laughed and shuddered as if she were cold.

"Do you miss the seasons, the snow and fall colors?"

She didn't have to think about his question. "I do. There's nothing like spending the holidays next to a roaring fire with cocoa or coffee and spending time with the family. I got home a couple of years ago, but flights are super expensive from mid-November until after the new year. I try to go up during spring break when this place starts to percolate. I used to rent out my house and I made enough in two weeks to pay the mortgage for two months."

"I had no idea. Your uncle isn't charging me much to stay here; he gave me a monthly rate."

"Well, he shouldn't be since there are officially two renters. It's like double-dipping." She unfolded her legs from under her and got up. "I need to get changed. What time do you want to go to the lighthouse?"

"An hour? I need to shower, and don't we need to make food?"

"We just need to pack the cooler." She looked at her computer. "I'll meet you in the kitchen in an hour."

He tapped his forehead with a salute. "It's a plan."

Kelly saved the project she was working on and locked her screen. If they got back early, she might work for another hour or two. The storm had put her behind schedule and even though her client would understand, she never liked to deliver anything late. That was one way to sour a customer and keep referrals low, and she wasn't going to take any chances with her business. This was also why she rarely took a vacation and when she did, the laptop went with her so she could work half days.

*W*hen she entered the kitchen, Tric was already filling the cooler. He looked yummy in a deep-green tee, boot cut jeans that hugged his backside just right, and sneakers. He glanced up.

"Double-check what I packed." He stopped and smiled as he drank her in, from her toes to her eyes. "You look great."

"So do you." She peeked into the soft-sided cooler and noted bottled water and a bottle of red wine propped upright. He had already uncorked it for easy opening once they got to the lighthouse.

They both reached for the handles at the same time. Their hands touched and they looked into each other's eyes.

She wanted to lace their fingers, but they had agreed to remain just friends. It was a shame, with so much chemistry between them.

She withdrew her hand, and he said, "I'll drive."

*T*ric paused near the entrance to the beach once they reached the parking area at the lighthouse. He wanted to say something profound. Instead, he said, "Ready?"

There was a family picnicking on the beach so they didn't have the space to themselves, but it wasn't like sitting in a restaurant where they'd be on top of anyone.

"We should walk down the beach," Kelly said as she bent over and took her shoes off.

He followed suit. "No sense getting them filled with sand."

She gave him a flick of sand with her toes and grinned. Even if conversation didn't flow like it had, he was determined to get it back on track with an easy and breezy topic. All of that was still between them which was evident by her playful grin. Too bad he didn't have one.

"We should drive past your house when we're done here. You'll be shocked to see how quickly things are going up."

She flashed him a smile. "I'd like that."

Well, at least he had said something right.

17

*W*ith his legs stretched out on the brightly striped blanket, Tric sipped his wine. Seagulls landed near them, hoping to steal a tasty morsel.

"Why do seagulls fly over the sea?"

Kelly gave him a lazy smile. "Lame jokes are back?"

"Hey, not all my jokes are bad." He winked. It was funny having someone to tell his oddball jokes to and she actually laughed. "Are you going to answer?"

She looked out over the water and seemed to be considering how to respond. She then looked back at him. "I don't know."

He waited half a beat and then in a deadpan tone, said, "If they flew over the bay, they would be bagels."

With a hoot of laughter, she said, "You have got to be kidding me."

Tric leaned closer. "Did you get the punchline?"

"Yeah, I did, but you really need to work on new material."

"I can do that during the drive to Chicago." He shook

his head. Now he'd done it. He'd brought up the touchy subject of leaving.

Moving on to a safer topic, he said, "What are you working on now? Still the candy shop website?"

She looked pleased he remembered. "No, that one's done until they get ready for international shipments, so that will be interesting. Now I'm working on an author website."

"Did the storm put you behind schedule?" He popped open a container of crackers and offered it to her.

"It's due Monday and I'll make the deadline."

How did she stay focused on her job even with the storm and him crashing her home? She was beyond gracious to walk with him every day and basically share her life with him. He looked up at the lighthouse. "I know how much you love history, so tell me the story of this impressive structure."

She nibbled on a slice of cheese and let the suspense tick up. "Like on all islands, being a lighthouse keeper was a lonely job. Back in the day when it was operational, the island was isolated. Then it was decommissioned mid-last-century, and they locked it up tight as a drum."

"That's it? No local legends?"

"There is one; a very bad hurricane sometime around nineteen hundred and that lighthouse"—she pointed to it for impact—"provided shelter for over one hundred islanders. The storm surge came up the iron steps, but the people huddled together in the stairwell and any available space there was, keeping each other safe throughout the storm. The lighthouse keeper had to turn the lens by hand since the winds were savage and prevented it from turning. For well over one hundred years, this lighthouse protected ships from running aground on all but a handful of nights."

"I couldn't imagine being a lighthouse keeper. It had to have been a lonely existence, but one that also needed a depth of courage most people don't possess."

With a thoughtful look, she said, "Some could say the same of your chosen career."

"I'm not lonely when fighting a wildfire. The team I work with is closer than brothers, and they are the most courageous men I've ever met."

He thought of them now. Would he ever find that again when he made the inevitable change? "Tell me more about why it was shut down. Was it because the building was deteriorating?"

"No. Shipping lanes were shifted away from the island, but after it was decommissioned, the historical society turned it into a tourist attraction, and they maintain it too. Then they added the pier to bring in even more people."

"The lighthouse dwarfs everything around here. It's good that it wasn't torn down but preserved."

She nodded. "I know. I hate it when old buildings are replaced with the shiny new in the name of progress." Giving him a sidelong look, she whispered, "It's reported to be haunted."

His brow cocked. She had captured his interest. Nothing like a good ghost legend to spice things up. "Do tell."

She placed a hand on her chest and opened her eyes wide. "I personally have never seen the ghost, but some tourists have said they see a flash out of the corner of their eye on the tour or even up at the top in the lamp area. Supposedly it's the figure of a man wearing old-fashioned clothes, watching the water, and some people even smell smoke from a cigar." She shrugged. "Until I see something with my own eyes, I'm not going to believe one way or the other."

"A skeptic. I can't say I disagree, but have you ever seen a ghost, anyplace?"

She tossed a seagull a cracker. "I've felt the occasional chill when I'm inside the lighthouse, but it might be from the breeze."

She was nonchalant about the subject of a resident ghost, so either she really didn't think there wasn't much to it or she'd had an experience and didn't want to talk about it.

Tric asked, "Do you like scary movies and Halloween?"

"The holiday or the movie franchise?" She sipped her wine as she studied him.

"The holiday, and scary movies in general."

"Yes to dressing up and passing out candy. No to movies that are even remotely scary, and I don't like blood, fake or real." She picked up a piece of cheese like she was holding up garlic to ward off a vampire. "Take that."

He chuckled. All he really wanted to do was sit close and share everything with her. Likes and dislikes of movies, books, vacation spots, even favorite cookies, but he wasn't going to be the one to complicate the arrangement they had come to. He had too much respect for her.

"What about you?"

"I like classic black-and-white vampire and werewolf movies and of course all Alfred Hitchcock flicks. The psychological thrillers were always the best."

"Give me a good comedy any day of the week." She licked her fingers and delicately picked up a cracker so as not to get sand on them.

He could feel a grin slide up one side of his face.

"Tell me about the woman who broke your heart."

Wow, that came out of the blue, and how did she know he had suffered a broken heart? "What do you mean? I never said I had a bad breakup."

"You must have. You haven't mentioned anyone since you got here and since we've, well, you know, gotten closer, I just know you're not the kind of man to have a fling, so what happened? I told you about my past. Now it's your turn."

Kelly was right. He knew that she had been cheated on and her heart had been broken before, and here she had let herself develop feelings for him, of that he was sure, and he needed to be completely honest with her.

"There was a woman that I was pretty serious with, but a relationship in my line of work is tough. The first year, it's great. Your girlfriend thinks she can handle you being gone for five months and lack of contact isn't that bad. But it turns out that for most women, those months are lonely, full of worrying about the person in the line of danger. So you come home from the job and she's happy to see you and you have a ton of time to spend with her. You get through the holiday season and as the weeks start to tick by and you've gone back into training mode to pass this year's endurance test, the conversation comes up about the danger, the months apart, the what-ifs. Soon the relationship takes a beating and crumbles under the strain and before you get back on the plane in June, you're single again. Basically, any romance is on a two-year cycle."

He looked out over the water and away from her sad eyes. Did she pity him or the woman left behind?

"I'm sorry it was hard for you and your ex-girlfriend. I can see both points of view. You're doing what you love

137

and her being lonely and dealing with the fear of you getting hurt. Were you single when you got hurt last fall?"

Her gentle tone touched that part of his heart that he had kept bandaged. "Yeah. We broke up almost a year ago."

"I'm sure that made it tough to not have someone special in your corner."

"Until I came here." When he spoke, it was without thinking and in his gut, he knew it was true. After all these weeks on the island, he was stronger physically and mentally than he thought possible, and he knew it was because of Kelly. He had drawn on her strength that first day walking on the beach. She challenged him to work hard without uttering a word. She kept their pace and it was Kelly who gave him the paper with the names of several gyms on the mainland, giving him everything he needed to push forward, even if she didn't realize it. The tranquility of the island had been what he had been searching for, but instead he had found far more than he had expected. When he got back home, he'd have to thank the chief for putting him in contact with Kevin.

They finished their picnic with pleasant conversation but nothing too deep. His last comment had summed up how he felt about her and what was left to say?

*K*elly was stunned speechless when he said those four words. He implied that she had helped him in his recovery. Too bad she had done such a good job; maybe he wouldn't want to leave. She reminded herself this had always been the plan—rest, recuperate, and then leave. Instead of dwelling on what was to come, she was enjoying his company now, although she wished she could renege on the agreement to be friends and nothing more. She wanted to fly across the blanket, pin him to the sand, and kiss him senseless—or let him take her in his arms and kiss her breathless. It didn't make any difference; she wanted to lock lips.

They were losing light and she still wanted to see the house construction.

"What do you say we pack it in for the day and head to my place?"

The glint in his eyes made her laugh.

"That sounded like a pickup line, but we both know my place is not ready for anything like that."

He held up his hands like he was innocent. "Did I say anything?"

"Tric." His name came out with a laugh. She tossed the cracker container at him. He caught it with one hand and placed it in the cooler.

He stood and pulled her up from the sand, then close to his chest. She could feel his breath on her cheek and smell the clean scent of his shirt, like the dryer sheets at the cottage. She took a step back and brushed an imaginary lock of hair off her face.

"We should, um, finish packing up." She would continue to deny the undeniable. She was more than attracted to him physically. She liked the entire package.

He cleared his throat. "Yeah, sure." He stashed everything in the cooler and helped her fold the blanket. He looked around. "Cigar smoke."

But there wasn't anyone near enough to them who was smoking. Kelly turned in a full circle. "Maybe it's the lighthouse keeper checking on us." She looked up at the lamp room and tugged on Tric's sleeve. "Look," she breathed. She pointed to the shadow figure of an old man at the top of the lighthouse. After all these years, she had finally seen the legendary ghost, and it was with Tric by her side.

"Well, now. Isn't that interesting? We've seen a ghost. I wonder if he has a message for us."

"Maybe he showed up to tell you the trip back to Chicago will be smooth sailing."

"Or maybe he's trying to tell us that the trip to your place"—he wiggled his eyebrows—"will be without slowdowns."

"Come on; let's get in the car and go see what the fuss is about at my place." She reached for the handle on the cooler, but he held it tight.

"A gentleman never lets his lady carry anything heavy if it can be avoided, and if you don't believe me, just ask my mom."

She held up her hands. "Okay. I'll let you carry the cooler." She tipped her head to the side and gave him a wide smile. "This time."

18

The last week and a half had been uneventful and had gone by too quickly. Kelly and Tric had taken a few bike rides and wandered around the pier again, but there was definitely an attempt on her part to put some distance between them. He got it. Self-preservation.

Tric gathered all his dirty laundry into two piles, lights and darks, and checked the time, wondering if it was too early to start the laundry. The sun was just barely up and he didn't want to wake Kelly. He wanted to leave with clean clothes and since it would be late when he got back to Chicago, he needed his lucky workout shirt for the test.

He heard a thump and a curse word. That question had been answered. He scooped up a load and walked with heavy steps down the hall into the main bathroom, which doubled as the laundry room. He could smell the fresh-brewed coffee and he pushed out of his mind that today was the last day he'd linger over a cup with Kelly. After he started the washer, he went into the kitchen and discovered she was sitting on the back deck, basking in the early morning sun. The reddish-gold highlights in her dark hair shimmered. His heart constricted. Was he making the wrong decision? Should he stay?

"I know you're hanging around in the kitchen. Are you coming out?" she called over her shoulder without turning to look at him.

"Want more coffee?"

She held up her mug and waved it from side to side. "Yes, please. I'm empty and I'll need a full pot to give me a burst of energy."

He took the pot out with him and refilled her mug before placing his on the small wooden table between their chairs.

"Good morning." She flashed him a smile, her eyes hidden behind her sunglasses.

"You're up early." The sun was bright and he wished he had grabbed his glasses too. He turned in his chair as the sun warmed his side.

"I have some updating and maintenance website work before I start working on a new project."

He nodded. "It's good that you're busy."

She sipped her coffee. "It pays the bills and once the house is done, I'll need to take some time off to move. Not that I have too much to pack, but there will be furniture to buy and all the mundane things like dishes and linens."

"That's a lot. Can't you order stuff online to make it easier?"

"I will, but I might take a day and head over to the mainland for a mall run. I can get most of what I need there, but for specialty items I'll check out some artisan shops online."

He wanted to say he'd help, but who knew where he'd

be when it came time for her to move. "You'll be in by May?"

"That's what Mike says." They sat in uncomfortable silence for several minutes.

"Tric, would you have dinner with me tonight?"

He wasn't even going to play around. Not this time. "Yes." He wanted to spend as much time as he could with her today, even though they both had a full day, him with getting ready to leave and her with work.

"What do you have planned?" She held the mug to her lips.

"Getting ready to go. Laundry, pack the car, and clean. I want to leave by seven thirty tomorrow."

With a catch in her voice, she said, "Oh." She turned away from him and went inside.

He didn't follow her, sensing she needed some space. He knew he needed a moment to suppress his emotions.

Through the open kitchen window, she said, "I'm making toast."

He heard her voice crack and his heart ached for both of them. "That'd be great. Need help?"

"No. Relax. In a few days, you'll be missing that view."

She was right, but it wasn't the ocean he'd miss the most. They were tap-dancing around the big polka-dot elephant. Their conversation was still pleasant, like it had been ever since the beginning of his stay with her, but at the same time something had shifted and there was a sadness to them both. Which one of them would speak their truth? He wanted to, but he had no right to tell her he had fallen for her and was still walking away.

She pushed the screen door open with her foot, and he hopped up and took the plates from her hands.

"Does anything else have to come out?"

"No. I hope you don't mind peanut butter and honey. We're out of jam."

It was a simple comment, but the inference of them as a duo felt like a red-hot spark in the heart.

"Honey's good." He gave her a small smile. "Are you okay?"

"Yeah, I'm fine. Just a lot on my mind."

He didn't push her, but said, "You know if you ever need anything, just call."

She looked at him, he thought, her sunglasses shrouding her eyes. "You too."

This was harder than he had expected. He was sure that to a casual observer, the situation looked like breakfast with the woman he cared for. Now, he was leaving in less than twenty-four hours.

She finished her breakfast. "Six o'clock for dinner?"

"Sounds good. Do you mind if we take your car? Mine will be packed."

"Yeah, sure." She swirled the last of her coffee before she drank it. "Off to work. The commute will be light today." She cracked a smile.

Her eyes grew bright as he got her joke. "Have a good day at the office."

"Thank you." She flicked her hair with a laugh. She opened the door and paused on the threshold. "By the way, you're on KP duty."

He touched his brow in a mock salute. "Yes, ma'am." He couldn't help but notice her eyes were bright with unshed tears, and he knew the last thing she wanted was for him to see them.

She hurried inside. It was apparent she was doing her best to keep things light, but it was agony for both of them. He hoped work would be a good escape for her.

. . .

*S*he could hear Tric walking up and down the hall. His steps were without a hitch, unlike when he had arrived. She heard the washer and dryer running and could picture him carrying his large duffel bag full of clean clothes to his car.

He tapped on her office door.

She swiveled in her chair and faced him.

"Hey, I'm running some towels. Want me to toss anything in with them?"

"No, thanks." She turned back to her computer and put her headphones on, blocking out the sounds of him preparing to leave her. Doing her own laundry would fill some of the quiet hours ahead of her in the next few days.

Was she fooling him with her nonchalant attitude, like it was no big deal he was leaving? More than likely not.

She thought about what she'd wear to dinner tonight. She wanted to look nice but not like she was trying too hard. The weather was warm so she could wear a skirt and be a little dressy.

She could feel him linger and then move away. He pulled her office door partially closed. Had he wanted to say something else?

She got up, work forgotten, but before she walked out of her office, she paused and listened. The house was quiet.

She pulled the door open and walked into the main living space. "Tric?" She didn't get a response. She crossed the room and opened the sliders to the front deck just in time to see his car pulling out of the driveway. Sinking to the chaise, she flopped back. The space was still shaded but before long, the sun would be directly overhead. A chill caused goosebumps to race over her bare arms.

She hit the arm of the chair and wiped tears from her cheeks. "Today sucks." But tomorrow would be worse. Then he would be gone.

*T*ric's first stop was to get an oil change and fill the gas tank. As he waited, he looked up the area florists and made a few calls. He had to find a very special plant. On his next to last call, he found what he wanted at a small store over near the bridge. Satisfied, he needed to get some notepaper and a small box of truffles.

He drove to one of his favorite spots. With the view of the lighthouse to his left and the ocean in front of him, it was time to write the hardest letter of his life.

Dear Kelly,

I want to thank you for taking a chance on a stranger, only on the word of your uncle, and letting me stay. I guess in hindsight it was lucky for me there wasn't anything available. Supported by your friendship and encouragement, my recovery progressed at a rapid pace, but it was more than that. For the first time, I felt a connection with another person at a profound level. This was totally unexpected and spending every day with you while at LCB has changed me forever.

Today is our last day together and I've hesitated to share what I'm feeling with you. Yes, it's one of my many flaws but hopefully none of them are fatal. I hesitate to share what is locked in my heart and now it has caused me to leave an important part of my life. Yes, you are very important to me. I was serious when I said if you ever need me, I'll be there for you.

Kel, I don't know what will happen a week from now, but I

do know how I'll feel about you a week, a month, or even a year from now. That won't change.

Once you get this letter, if you want to take a chance and tempt the luck of the Irish at the same time next year, all you have to do is reach out. You are my anam cara. You will always be with me.

Tric

He watched the water a while longer before driving around the coast road one final time. He had a couple of hours before dinner and he didn't have anything left to do and didn't want to just hang around even though he'd be closer to Kelly. He wanted to take a few pictures to show his mom the place that felt like home, and he even wanted to take pictures of Kelly's home under construction since Dad wasn't going to believe he had swung a hammer, even if it was on the sly. Maybe he'd make more time to help around the family cottage this spring.

He returned to the house and jogged up the stairs, leaving the small tokens of his affection in the car. He'd grab them after dinner. What a difference now. He felt great—physically, at least.

When he walked into the cottage, Kelly was sitting at the kitchen table. His mind went blank. She looked so beautiful and it hit him in the gut; he was going to miss her more than he had missed any other woman before.

"Hi. Did you get everything done for your trip?"

"Yeah. You look beautiful." He wanted to kiss her cheek but refrained.

"Thank you." She flushed. "Do you still want to go at six?"

"It won't take me long to get cleaned up. Give me fifteen minutes?"

"Take all the time you need."

. . .

*K*elly and Tric walked into the restaurant. His hand rested lightly on the small of her back. They saw an open booth and sat down.

After they ordered, Tric looked around. "So, this is where you'll come to have St. Paddy's Day dinner?"

"For one night, everyone in Last Chance Beach becomes Irish and this space is transformed. There'll be an Irish band, food, and plenty of beer."

"Sounds like it'll be a lot of fun. Too bad my tests came up so quickly. I would have liked to have been here with you."

"Maybe another time." Her eyes were bright.

Their draft beers were delivered. They tapped glasses and took a drink. He wished he could say he'd be back soon. Who knew for sure how things would work out, but if there was any possible way, he would be back.

"Yeah, another time."

19

---

*T*he next morning, Kelly was in the kitchen before Tric made his way down the hall. She moved around the room and made coffee and set the table for breakfast.

This was the last chance she'd have to prank Tric, and she hoped it would play out perfectly. In the middle of the night, she snuck out of bed and poured cereal and milk in a bowl and hidden it in the freezer behind the vegetables just in case he went looking for a late-night snack.

She was casually leaning against the counter sipping her coffee when he walked in the kitchen. "Good morning." She gave him a bright smile.

"You're up early."

"I wanted to make breakfast for you." She poured coffee into a mug and handed it to him. "You mentioned you wanted to have a light meal, so I thought we'd have cereal and fruit."

"That'll work." He pulled out a chair and he picked up the newspaper she had left in his chair before he sat down.

She got the milk and cereal box out of the cabinets and

refrigerator and made a show of pouring some into a bowl and adding milk. Before she walked over, she double-checked to make sure he was still distracted when she snuck the frozen bowl of cereal and milk out of the freezer. She carried it along with the normal bowl to the table. Setting her bowl down, she then placed the special bowl in front of Tric. He didn't look down but picked up his spoon and went to dig in. The spoon clattered against the frozen milk.

He let out a snort. "Is this my breakfast?"

She kept her face expressionless. "Yes. I thought you liked shredded wheat."

"Well, I do, but I like the milk cold and the cereal soggy."

"Give it some time. It'll get that way eventually." She kept her voice even and smothered the laugh that wanted to burst out.

He clapped his hands together. "Why, Kelly O'Malley, I think I've turned you into a jokester."

She gave a nonchalant shrug. "Guess I was paying attention."

She gave him a hard hug, promising herself she wasn't going to cry. She waited until she could form a sentence. "The door is always open if you ever want to come back for a vacation or whatever. I'll have plenty of room."

He tightened his arms around her and whispered, "I don't know when, but I *will* be back."

She nodded and blinked away the tears that threatened to fall. "I'm glad I didn't smack you with the skillet the day we met."

His laugh was low. "A first impression I'll never forget." He kissed her forehead. "See you sometime."

She was glad he didn't say goodbye. That was oh, so final.

He picked up his small bag; the rest of his things were already in the car. She walked down the wide stairs clutching his hand, their agreement forgotten.

He tossed the bag in the back, cupped her cheeks, and hesitated until she slipped her hand around the back of his neck. Tenderly, he brushed his mouth across her lips. There were no words that could convey more than his slow, tender kiss.

With the back of her hand, she wiped his face of her tears, which had combined with his.

She stepped from his embrace. "May the sun shine warm upon your face until we meet again."

He kissed her one final time and got into the car. He lifted his hand and pulled out of the driveway. She waved as he made the final turn onto the street.

*W*ith a heavy heart, Kelly climbed the stairs to Shamrock Cottage. When she walked inside, the space felt empty, like its heartbeat had just stopped and she didn't know CPR to get it restarted. So much for the Shamrock being lucky.

It would be good when her house was finished. Memories of Tric wouldn't be around every corner. She walked into her office and stopped. Sitting in the middle of her desk was a potted shamrock plant. There was an envelope propped against it. Her heart quickened and she took the note and walked out to the deck overlooking the water before she sat down to read.

His handwriting was bold. It matched who he was— courageous and confident. As she read his heartfelt words, she placed her hand over her heart and swallowed the lump that had lodged in her throat.

As she read the note again, she wished she had a second chance. He should have spoken up and told her what was in his heart. Instead, she was having to read between the lines, but she knew he cared for her just as deeply as she did for him. But why did she have to wait a year? Did he think she might not have strong feelings for him and absence would make her heart grow fonder? What was wrong with him? He was such a guy… She groaned. She wasn't any better, letting him leave without being honest. They were a great pair, both running from their hearts.

As she read the last two sentences again, she said, "*Anam cara*? What does that mean?"

She hurried into her office and sat down at the computer. She rapidly typed in those two words in a search engine. When the results appeared, she sucked in a breath. "Soulmates."

She grabbed her phone from her back pocket. Her fingers hovered over the screen. He wouldn't even have gotten to the bridge yet. If she called him now, would he turn around without going back for his tests? That was not something she wanted to stop. If they were meant to be together, well then, fate would have to step in and give their floundering romance a hand.

She carefully folded the note and put it back in the envelope. She was going to save it since this was the first love letter she had ever received—except for the one in the fifth grade, from Bobby whatever his last name was. It had been the last day of school before summer and he gave her a note asking if she'd be his girlfriend, and then poof! His family up and moved the next week. The similarities of the situation were not lost on her.

She was going to give Tric space for the next couple of weeks and let him get through whatever he needed to do. At some point, either she'd call him or he'd call her and they would talk. If his passion was to be a smoke jumper, then she would support it. She'd never squelch his dream, and if that was the course of his future and they still wanted something together, they'd work it out. This might have been *see you*, but it wasn't goodbye.

 ric took the long way around the island before driving over the bridge. His heart was still at the cottage with Kelly, and this was an unfamiliar emotion for him. He had never regretted leaving someone before, even when he thought he had been in love with the woman.

Once he was back on the mainland, he got on the highway and headed north. As the miles clicked by, the sun rose higher in the sky and his leg began to ache a bit. It was almost like leaving didn't just hurt his heart but was also causing him physical discomfort.

Turning his thoughts to the tasks ahead of him, he wanted to make it back to Chicago in two days, but that would be tough when he still needed to stop and move every couple of hours. He resigned himself to driving as long as he could each day, and it would take as long as it took.

He cranked up some classic rock and roll as the miles rolled, taking him farther away from Kelly and the only place that had felt like home since he moved out of his parents' house.

He needed to stay focused. Passing the physical first and then the endurance test. He knew it would be arduous and more than half of his success would depend on being able to dig deep. The mental fortitude it took to be a smoke jumper was something many recruits overlooked. Each year, a jumper had to requalify for fitness; only the best could be on the front lines.

He thought of the jump that had caused the injury. There wasn't anything he could have done at the time to prepare for what had turned out to be the worst-case scenario and still survive. The wind had changed with such intensity and the landing spot had no longer been an option. He was lucky. It could have been so much worse. In looking at the risks more objectively, he could understand why Alyssa had broken it off with him. He wouldn't want to be the one at home waiting for a phone call. For the first time, he contemplated how his mother must feel when he left. Her kids were everything to her and even now, their hurts were hers.

But the country needed people like him, willing to take the risk, to put life and limb on the line to protect the land and the wildlife that lived within it. That was why he did it, not like the guys who really were jacked on the danger.

He began to walk through each step in the process of the endurance test. There were always slight variables like September.

His team had been awesome. With speed and efficiency, they had him stabilized and strapped to the gurney, ready for the helicopter to do the pickup. In between each checkpoint on the hike out of the woods, he had been in and out of it. Damn, he had never felt that kind of agony before.

After several long hours of driving, he decided to stop for a decent lunch and to stretch. He wanted to call Kelly, to see how she was, but would that send a mixed message? He'd call her when he got back to Chicago, just to let her know he had arrived.

Up ahead were signs for a steakhouse, Italian, fast food, and a mini-mart. Something hearty would hit the spot. He chuckled when he thought of his frozen cereal. That was a good prank, and one he wouldn't have thought of. He'd have to put on his thinking cap for the next time he was with Kelly. Payback was going to be fun.

*A*fter a fourteen-hour day spent behind the wheel of the car and all that windshield time watching the landscape change, Tric couldn't get his mind off the woman he loved. He would see something and want to call and tell her about it, would hear a song on the radio and remember how she would hum or sing in her office to whatever she was streaming as it played softly in the background.

It had been one day, one very long, lonely day without talking or even just being under the same roof as her. He had officially turned into a sap. As other members of his team had left to settle down and have a family, he had never gotten it when they explained about the person who gave them that sense of being happy in one place. They had gone on to be city firemen, emergency medical techs, and policemen.

There was a sign for a hotel up ahead and he needed to get a hot shower to ease out some of the stiffness from driving, sleep in a bed, and start early tomorrow. If he hit the road early enough, he'd be sleeping in his own bed very late tomorrow night.

*T*he house was silent. No sounds of Tric getting ready for bed. Dinner for one had been lonely, which had never bothered Kelly until now. How could she have let him turn her world upside down so easily and so fast? Tomorrow would be a better day; she'd get back to her routine and maybe even go shopping for living room furniture. Plan for the future and forget about the handsome dark-haired man with the deep dimples and quick smile who now invaded her every thought. Her phone rang and her heart skittered in her chest.

"Hi."

"Hey, Kel. How's it going?"

Her stomach flipped and her breath quickened. "Good. Where are you?"

"At the halfway point. I just checked into a hotel and wanted to give you a call."

Her heart clenched. "I found your note and the plant. Thank you. It was very sweet of you."

"I'm glad." He paused. Was he waiting for her to talk about the note? She wasn't ready.

"I'm going to hit the shower and then bed. Another long day tomorrow, but we'll talk soon?"

"Sounds like a plan. Good night, Tric."

"'Night, Kel."

Hearing his voice made her soul ache. Who was she kidding? He had wormed his way into her heart. So much for avoiding love.

20

_____

a few days later, Tric was waiting at the medical center, ready for his fitness for duty physical. Tomorrow was the big day. He was the only person there this early. Being home was bittersweet. He missed Kelly and Last Chance Beach, but he was enjoying time with his family. His parents had been happy to have a quiet dinner for them and his gran, and he told them all about the last two months, including a brief mention of Kelly. Then it was a family affair; his brothers and sister and their families, along with a few aunts and uncles, all showed up for an early St. Patrick's Day celebration since his dad thought it would bring him luck with his test. At least the weather was going to cooperate, with sunny skies, cooler temps, and zero snow in the forecast, so his run would be smooth as silk.

Time after time he reached for the phone to call Kelly. Other than a brief conversation the day after he got home, they hadn't spoken. He longed to hear about everything she was doing, but she couldn't get off the phone fast

157

enough. He'd been crushed but if she was hurting as much as he was, well, he got it.

Who was he kidding? In some ways, he had hoped it wouldn't be like that so he wouldn't have to miss her even more, but it hadn't worked. He longed to see her soft-gray eyes, which held a hint of mischief, and feel the weight of her hand in his.

A man wearing scrubs appeared in the waiting room. "Patrick Ryan, would you come with me, please?" Over his shoulder, he said, "I saw you got your bloodwork done before today. Thank you."

"I'm anxious to be released for duty."

The man didn't respond to Tric's statement and gestured for him to enter an exam room. He took his pulse, blood pressure, weight, and temperature before saying, "Dr. Matthews will be in soon."

A stack of old magazines was sitting next to the sink and Tric picked one up and thumbed through it.

There was a quick tap on the door and his doctor came in and shook his hand. "Tric, good to see you again." He gave him the once-over. "You look good so far." He took a seat on a rolling stool. "Tell me. How are you feeling?"

"Really good. I spent a few weeks down south at the beach. I did a lot of walking and running, worked out, and soaked up the rays. It was good for me."

"I can see that you're down a few pounds." He consulted the laptop screen. "Your bloodwork looks excellent." He looked up. "How's your stress level? Concerned about tomorrow?"

It was like that with Dr. Matthews; he kept his finger on the pulse of any smoke jumpers who came through the medical center and there were a few from the greater Chicago area.

Tric nodded. "I'm in a good place. I feel stronger than ever. The gym paid off in spades."

"What about up here?" He tapped his forehead. "The actual injury will heal, but the mental aspect of recovery is another major component. Any hesitation to get back in the line of fire, literally?"

Other than leaving the woman he loved? "No. I'm ready to roll."

Dr. Matthews watched him carefully and tapped the keyboard. "Let me take a look at you and if everything looks good, I'll release you for tomorrow's fun and games."

Tric liked how he made it seem like it was no big deal when both of them knew differently. This was his life, his future. Either way he had an important decision to make, and he wanted Kelly to be a significant part of whatever it might be.

*T*ric was relieved when he finally walked out of the medical center. He was cleared—medically, at least. He was going to go for an easy run before heading back to his place to get a few things done, and he wanted to ask his parents to have dinner with him tomorrow night. It no longer mattered if he passed or failed. Either way, he'd want company to celebrate or commiserate with.

He called his mom.

Right after they exchanged hellos, she asked, "How did the physical go?"

"I passed with flying colors, which is why I'm calling. I'd like to take you and Pop out for dinner tomorrow night, my treat."

"Just come here and save your money."

He smiled. She was always trying to save her kids money. "Nope. If you want to have dinner with your favorite single son, it's dinner out. I was thinking we'd go to the Chop House." It was where his family had always gone for celebrations. "What do you say? I'll make reservations for six thirty."

"That sounds nice and we'll meet you there so shoot me a text if the time changes."

"Perfect. See you then."

He jogged to the parking lot. He had decisions to make. Plan A, and he needed a plan B too.

*T*he next morning, Tric was awake by five. He never slept well before his requalification cert, but this year, he had a lot more riding on it. Today would change the course of his future forever, and no matter what, he wanted it to be on his terms. But he had to know if he could pass this test.

He showered and ate a decent breakfast but skipped the coffee and drank a lot of water to stay well hydrated since he had learned over the years that hydration was key.

His cell rang. Curious, he looked at the caller ID. His family had checked in last night to wish him good luck.

"Kelly, hey." He couldn't contain his grin and even if she couldn't see it, maybe she'd know by the sound of his voice that he was thrilled to hear hers.

"Hi, Tric. I wanted to wish you good luck today. I know you have a lot riding on it."

Her voice was soft and sweet to his ears. "It's good to hear from you." He sat down on a stool at the breakfast bar. He glanced around the space and wished she was sitting next to him.

"It's been a little over a week since we've talked. How've you been?" she asked.

"Good. Spending a lot of time at the gym and with the family. You know how big families are, any reason to have a party."

She laughed softly. "I do. I've been thinking of a trip to Boston this summer to see the folks. You sound good. Relaxed."

"As much as I can be. I passed my physical." He pushed his glass of water in a circle. "How's the house coming?"

"Funny story. Mike brought in another crew, so they're moving right along. I'll be in a month earlier than expected so I've been shopping for all the necessities. Uncle Kevin can get this place rented and make some money again. It's time to get my own life back to normal."

"I hear ya. It's hard to enjoy life when things are out of whack."

Like him missing her. It was harder now than it had been last week.

They both grew quiet. He wasn't sure what to say other than he missed her like crazy, but that was not a conversation for now. She hadn't given any indication she was missing him other than being a friend and wishing him good luck today.

"Well, if you get a chance later, let me know how things go."

Her voice was soft and breathy and it drew him in like oxygen feeding the flame. "I will definitely call you."

"Tric?"

His breath caught. "Yeah, Kel?"

After a long pause, she said, "You're gonna do great today. I know it."

"That means a lot and I'm glad you called. It was good to hear your voice."

"Right back at ya."

Did he hear a sniffle? "Are you okay?"

"Sure, I'm fine. Well, I need to start the day. Computer wizardry waits for no one."

Unconvinced that she wasn't crying, he decided to let her off the hook. "Thanks again."

After they said their quick goodbyes, he paced the room. Had he just missed another opportunity with her? He picked up his cell and put it back down. He'd call her later just like she had asked and over dinner, he was going to ask his parents for their advice.

a short time later, Tric parked his car at the fire department's training center. It had been used as the testing center for smoke jumpers in recent years since it had the towers and obstacle courses. The parking lot was partially filled with vehicles. Today wasn't just his day to get qualified; it was the day for lots of potential jumpers.

He carried a duffel bag of gear into the building, pleased to be greeted by a hum of voices growing louder with friendly banter. As he rounded the corner, he saw a few of his buddies and new faces too. He held up his hand in greeting to his uncle, John Bannon, who oversaw some of the testing and was the chief of the station.

The chief crossed the room to join Tric.

"Good to see you, Uncle John."

The chief gave him a half hug, a handshake, and a slap

on the back. "The beach looks like it agreed with you. How did everything work out with Kelly?"

"Good. No issues."

His eyebrow arched. "Did she come north with you?"

That was an odd question. "No. She's working on a couple of websites and rebuilding her house after her fire late last year."

"Kevin told me about that, but at least you got to meet her and had someone to show you around the island while you were there."

"She's great." He shifted his weight from foot to foot and looked around the registration area. "I should get at it so I can ace this test."

"Like the confidence." He gave his shoulder a squeeze. "You've got this, Tric."

"Appreciate the support, Chief."

He stood in line behind a guy he'd never seen before. A rookie.

The guy turned to him. "You're a first-timer?"

"Veteran. Been jumping a long time but I was on the injured list so I want to requalify to make sure I'm up to the job." Tric shook his head. He felt for the guy. "The nerves are the same for everyone. Just don't let them get to you."

"Thanks. I appreciate that."

The guy went to the right and Tric moved to the left. He was itching to get started after giving his name and confirming his personal stats. All this waiting around was a way to either kill the nerves or ramp them up. In some ways, it matched what happened when you were getting ready to face the fire-breathing dragon in the wild. He remembered his very first wildfire and walking into that hell. One of his rookie buddies had named it the dragon and it stuck, even all these years later.

He was handed a number to attach to his jacket sleeve and the forty-five-pound pack he'd be wearing on his back. With a quick change into his Kevlar-padded work pants and jacket, helmet and work boots, he was ready for the Work Capacity Test. He was going for the arduous pack test—no guts, no glory. For him, passing the test was all that mattered. He had one shot at it and the pack was sure to put a strain on him since he had trained without that in the last few weeks, but muscle memory was strong and he was mentally prepared to push through. The only thing he had to prove was to himself.

*L*ater in the day Tric sat at a table at the Chop House, waiting for his parents. He had gotten there a few minutes before six and had a frosty mug of beer in front of him. It had been an emotional day. Now all he had to do was talk to Mom and Dad and take the next step for his future.

His mom waved as she crossed the dining room with Dad behind her. He rose to his feet, a little sore from the day but overall better than he had expected.

She kissed his cheek, and he shook Dad's hand.

"Glad you said you'd come." Tric sat back in his chair and stretched his aching leg under the table.

Mom said, "Patrick, don't hold us in suspense any longer. Did you pass the test?"

He held their looks for a few moments, letting the tension build until it looked like his mom was about to burst with anticipation.

"You know it's a pass-fail and I was quite a bit older than a lot of the rookies."

"Tric."

He could hear the impatient tone in his dad's voice. He grinned. "I passed. But…"

"It's just what you wanted." Then his mom took a long look at him and he caught the look that lingered between his parents. "Is there more?" she asked.

"I had my personal best for time, but I don't want to go back to fighting wildfires. It's time for a change. I'm going back to Last Chance Beach to see if I can have a future with the only woman I can't get off my mind."

21

When Kelly's cell phone rang, she hoped it was Tric. His test had been today and she was waiting on pins and needles to know how he did. Relief flooded through her as she answered. "Hey there. I was wondering when you might call."

With a friendly hello, his voice didn't betray any emotion. The news could be good or bad. Her stomach clenched, steeling herself for the bad news. "I just got home from dinner with my parents."

"How's everyone? Good?" She really wasn't into making small talk, but it seemed like it might take some time to discover what had happened today.

"They're great. I took them out for steak at their favorite restaurant, and you know how moms are. She didn't want me to pick up the check. I swear she thinks they still need to pay for us kids, but of course I let them leave the tip."

"That was sweet of you. Your parents raised you right."

"That's a nice thing to say." He cleared his throat. "I have news."

"Do tell." She leaned closer to the phone as if she were leaning into him.

"I passed the test."

Her heart sank but she forced her tone to be upbeat. "That's great news. You have to be relieved to have that behind you."

"I am, and the next step is four weeks of conditioning training, but that won't start until Monday."

Her heart sank to her toes. Even though she was happy for him, that also meant there was no chance he would be coming back to LCB and to her. "I'm so happy for you, Tric."

"I can never thank you enough for all that you did for me. I am certain I wouldn't have been able to pass it if you hadn't been by my side, walking and jogging every day."

"It was nothing, but it was good motivation to get me off my butt and start moving. In fact, I've kept it up since you left."

"That's great news. Have you bumped into any more ghosts?"

She could hear the laughter in his voice. "Not yet, just the old man in the lighthouse and to be honest, one ghost is enough for me."

"I hear ya on that one." He wasn't sure if she wanted to hear about the test, but he said, "All the hard work paid off and I wanted to share. I clocked my best ever and that's thanks to you. I know it's just a pass or fail, but for me, achieving my personal best was something I hadn't expected."

"Congratulations." The word sounded hollow to her ears and hopefully he didn't pick up on it.

"You sound tired. Is everything okay there?"

She tossed her hair over her shoulder and put a smile on her face, remembering that she had read once that when you talked on the phone, your facial expression was picked up in your voice.

"I'm tired. Shopping for furniture and other household goods is exhausting." She really longed to hear him say he was coming back to the beach before he left for training, but that was just silly. He had other things to take care of. He'd been gone from his family for months, and would be again, and she was sure he wanted to spend all the time he could with them.

"So, I mentioned I'm going to visit my family over the July Fourth holiday. Take in the fireworks at the Esplanade next to the Charles River and listen to the Boston Pops." She wasn't sure why she blurted that out, but it seemed like a good idea in the moment.

"That sounds nice. I've never done that before."

Lightly, she said, "Add it to your bucket list. Everyone needs to go one time in their lives."

"Maybe sometime I could go with you and we could go to the North End for some Italian and play tourist."

"Yeah, that would be fun." Did he take her answer as totally noncommittal, or maybe it wouldn't faze him?

"Then we'll have to make it happen." A short pause followed. "Well, I'll let you go for tonight. Sleep well."

"You too. Bye."

He didn't disconnect and then said, "See ya."

After the line went silent, she exhaled. She was happy to hear his voice, but she was disappointed with the news he wasn't coming back anytime soon. Who knows, maybe after the fire season was over he'd be back. She straightened her shoulders and walked to the front deck. The sun had set and the stars were peeking out. Kelly felt more alone tonight than she had since he left.

It was time to refocus, call up her friends, and make plans for St. Patrick's Day. There was nothing like a little music, good food, and better friends to lift her spirits.

*A*fter Tric hung up from talking with Kelly, he was restless. He prowled around his condo. It was a nice place, but the walls were still contractor white. A few family photos decorated tabletops, and other than a good recliner and a large screen television hanging on the wall, it was like anyone might live here. The place had no personality. The neighborhood was good and the value must have gone up in the ten years since he bought it. The only thing that had gotten any regular use was the laundry room and the office, where he had set up exercise equipment. Nothing that couldn't be replaced.

His parents had been very supportive of his leaving Chicago and relocating. The only thing his mom had asked was for him to bring Kelly to the cottage at some point during the summer season. That was the easy part. Now she just had to agree to give them a real chance to have a future together.

Tomorrow he'd go see his uncle and let him know about the changes he was making and maybe even see if he could talk to Kevin and thank him personally for renting the cottage to him.

It was dumb luck how things had turned out. If it hadn't been for that mix-up, he would never have met his soulmate. Hell, two months ago, he hadn't even believed in such a thing. He shot a text off to Uncle John, telling him he'd swing by the station tomorrow. He had news.

. . .

*I*t was almost ten when Tric got to the station after a quick stop at the donut shop for coffee and dozens of today's special creations. If there was one thing he had learned, it was to never go to the firehouse without both.

Some of the squad was washing down the trucks and waxing them and others were checking equipment and restocking any necessary supplies. It was a never-ending job.

When one of his buddies noticed him, he called out, "Tric, what's happening?"

He held aloft the coffee jug and boxes. "I thought you guys might need a pick-me-up."

With a chorus of thanks, he was relieved of both in short order.

"Is my uncle upstairs?"

"The chief should be in the kitchen."

He ran up the stairs to the second floor which housed the kitchen along with the sleeping quarters and game room, following the aroma of onions sautéing.

"Tric, how the heck are ya today? You should be pretty pumped after yesterday."

"I am." Uncle John handed him a peeler and a five-pound bag of carrots.

He took them, washed his hands, tied on a black chef's apron, and got to work. "What's on the menu today?"

"Stew. Something to stick to the ribs. You're welcome to have dinner with us tonight."

"Thanks, but I have a few things to do."

He made short work of the carrots before the chief said, "What's on your mind?"

Tric gave him a side-look before cleaning up his workspace.

"You're only quiet this long when you have something to get off your chest."

The man who was like his second father waited patiently as he browned the stew meat. Tric knew from experience he could wait out the best procrastinator.

"Thanks for being at the test yesterday. It was good to see a friendly face."

"It was nothing."

"It was important to me." He cleared his throat. "Which is why I wanted to talk to you. I've decided to change careers. Don't get me wrong; I wanted to take the test and pass it so I could go out on my own terms. Over the last few weeks, I've discovered I want a different life."

The chief assessed him with his normal keen eye. "What are you thinking?"

"I'm going back to Last Chance Beach to ask Kelly if she has feelings for a retired smoke jumper and let the embers of what I think is between us ignite."

He clapped Tric on the back. "All I can say is that is the best news I've heard in a long time. But what is it about this girl that's so special?"

"You might think this sounds cheesy, but everything."

"Ah, now I get it. It's the same way I felt when I met your aunt. I'd walk through fire for that woman."

He clapped his hand on the counter. "Exactly."

"Congratulations. I'm happy things are working out the way I'd hoped."

"What are you talking about?" Now Tric was confused. How was the chief involved in his feelings for Kelly?

"Confession over a beer after shift change? I can meet you at O'Brien's at seven."

His mouth fell open. "You're gonna leave me hanging?"

He shook his head. "I gotta make a phone call first, and then I'll explain."

"Doesn't sound like you're going to spill it now, so I'll meet you later. Oh, and can you give me Kevin's phone number? I'd like to call him and say thanks for renting me the cottage."

With a shrug, he said, "Sure. I can do that tonight too."

"Catch you later. Oh, and I brought donuts and coffee. On my way out, I'll ask one of the guys to bring you one. Today was the leprechaun special."

He rolled his eyes. "One of my favorites."

"Chief, who are you trying to kid? You like all donuts." Tric slapped his shoulder and gave it a squeeze. "Catch you later."

He left the firehouse with a lot to do. He was going to surprise Kelly and make it back to Last Chance Beach by March seventeenth.

22

———

It was the day before St. Patrick's and Tric had made it back to the beach. He rented a motel room on the mainland so he could finish making plans to surprise Kelly at The Sandbar. He had missed her something fierce and could already feel her in his arms.

After a quick trip to the gym to work out in the morning, he'd double-checked the time the festivities got underway and hoped she was still planning on going. It would be a huge letdown if he didn't find her there. But for now, he fell onto the bed, exhausted from the two-day marathon driving session. The next time they went north, they'd have to do it in three days and enjoy the journey. But when he thought about it, with Kelly sitting next to him, the trip would sail by.

Kelly came in from her run on the beach and drank some water before checking emails and social media. Tric had been strangely silent since he

LUCINDA RACE

passed his test, but she guessed he was getting ready to leave for training. She'd hoped he would have come back down at least for a few days, but she hadn't suggested it. Too bad he was going to miss tonight; St. Patrick's Day would have been a lot more fun with him. Maybe their time had washed away like the tide.

There was an email from the cabinet shop about an issue with some of the hardware she'd chosen. Instead of sending a response, she called them. She was enjoying the joys of building her home and instead of the devil being in the details in this case, it was the mischievous leprechaun at play. She was having a blast putting her personal stamp on her place. When she had gone over last night, she was happy to walk through the rooms and see how fast things were changing daily. She could imagine what each room would look like with furniture in place, photos hanging on the walls, and the views on both sides, one looking over the island and the other with a glimpse of the ocean. Almost perfect. It was just too bad she had lost all her mementos in the fire. But things could be replaced. She was even thinking of rescuing a senior kitty for some companionship. Living with Tric for those short weeks had reminded her about connections and the importance of interacting, even if it was with a bundle of fur. There would be time to check into pet adoption once she got settled.

Her phone pinged with a text reminder to meet her friends tonight for the St. Paddy's extravaganza at The Sandbar. A part of her wanted to stay holed up at the cottage but the other part needed to be with people.

Hey, Judy. See you at six thirty, and don't forget to wear your green! Go Irish!

She turned her attention to what she was going to wear. Something pretty to help shake off the funk that had woven its way around her, and she had the perfect dress and jewelry. *You need to dress up for the night even if you're taking yourself out.*

She wandered into her bedroom and flung open the closet. Thank heavens her favorite dress had been at the cleaners. She pulled a hanger from the rod. Her shamrock dress was ready to wear. Next, she selected matching high-heeled emerald-green sandals, and the final touch would be her jewelry. With a smile, she opened the box and withdrew the unique item no other woman would have on tonight. Satisfied, she laid it on top of the dresser, glanced in the mirror, and grinned at her reflection. Too bad Tric hadn't stuck around. She was going to look smokin' hot tonight.

*T*ric entered The Sandbar just before seven. He knew the bar opened a half hour ago, but he wanted to give Kelly time to arrive and relax, since she liked to be punctual. But he wondered if he could sneak in and see if she had come with a man before he surprised her. His heart thudded in his chest and he could feel his shoulders sag. It would be awkward if she was on a date, even if it was casual.

If he could have smacked himself on the forehead without looking like he was nuts, he would have. He was a dumb jerk; she could date whoever and whenever she wanted. He had never said he loved her and what his plan was. He had left to see what his future held, and she had no idea it was with her.

And then he saw her.

Kelly was stunning in a short-sleeved emerald-green dress that clung to her curves and flared from her waist to her knees. She had on high-heeled shoes in a deep shade of green that matched her dress and showed off her sculpted legs to perfection, and then he covered his grin. She was holding back her long, dark hair with a crown of silver and crystal shamrocks. A touch of whimsy to coordinate with a pretty dress on an even more beautiful woman.

He didn't move across the room to greet her but stood to one side of the bar and ordered a Guinness. He reached for the pint glass the bartender handed him and took a drink. A smile tipped his mouth as he watched her. She glanced around the room as if searching for something or someone until their eyes met.

Her mouth went slack and her eyes widened. She handed her beer to the girl she had been talking to and crossed the room, her eyes locked on him.

His name came out as an exhale. "Tric."

He took her in his arms and kissed her as she melted into him. A few toe-curling kisses later, reluctantly he eased her from his chest.

"Kelly." He traced the curve of her cheek. Her skin was as soft as he remembered, and her musky perfume caused his heart to skip and quicken in his chest. "You look gorgeous."

"Thank you, but what are you doing here? And why didn't you tell me you were coming?"

He curled his arm around her waist, reveling in being close to her. "Happy to see me?"

Her eyes sparkled. "Did you happen to miss that kiss?"

He slowly shook his head. "Nope."

She placed a hand over his heart. "You look good. When did you get here?"

"I stayed across the bridge last night. I wanted to surprise you." He brushed his lips across her cheek and held her tighter as a shiver raced over her. "How did I do?"

"Totally caught me off guard." She tugged his hand. "Come meet my friends."

He grabbed his glass and allowed her to guide him to the other side of the room, where a group of six people were sitting at a table, a few of them drinking beer, one a glass of wine, and the rest seemed to be drinking whiskey.

"Everyone, this is my friend Tric, whom I was telling you about, and Tric, this is everyone."

He waved a hand at the group. "It's nice to meet you all. I hope you don't mind if I crash the party."

The band struck the first chord and Kelly gave him a grin. "Dance with me?"

He clasped her hand with a gentle squeeze. "I thought you'd never ask."

The tenor crooning, driving beat of the fiddles, and the trill of the tin whistle with the thrum of the guitar was hypnotic. It cast a spell over him. He swayed Kelly in his arms. Her smile melted away any reservations he had experienced on the drive here. They had much to talk about, but tonight was for fun.

*K*elly laughed as she twirled in Tric's arms until she didn't think she could dance another step. She waved a hand in front of her overheated face. "Water."

"And dinner? The buffet is ready." He pointed over his shoulder.

Butterfly wings fluttered in her stomach. She was curious why he had come back to LCB, and when did he have to leave?

She filled two glasses with water from the pitcher at the end of the bar before ordering two beers. Carrying a small tray for the glasses, they crossed to the buffet and filled their plates before finding an empty table for two.

Looking at him warmed her heart. It was so good to see him sitting across the table. She waited until she just had to ask, "Are you going to tell me what's going on? I never expected to see you tonight."

"When I left, something vital to me was left behind and I had to come back for it. I couldn't take my next step without it."

"I would have shipped it to you and saved you the trouble."

He cut his potato in two halves and put one half on her plate.

She looked at him, not masking her confusion.

"My granny told me a long time ago it is easy to halve a potato where there is love."

For a moment, she let his comment sink in. "Are you saying you want to share the potato with me?"

He took her hand. "I hadn't even gotten over the bridge and I knew leaving you was the hardest thing I've ever done."

She dropped her eyes. "You had to go back; you had responsibilities. I get that."

"I did have to go home, but not for all the reasons you think. But before I go any further, I have to know how you felt when I left."

She looked across the room. What the heck; she was going to put her heart on the line. If he stepped on it, he could only bruise it. It would heal.

"I waved until I couldn't see your car any longer and I kept telling myself I should have asked you to stay." She looked him straight in the eye. "Would you have said yes?"

23

*E*ric pulled his chair closer to Kelly and took both her hands in his, holding them firmly and with warmth pouring into her.

"As much as I wanted to stay, there were things I had to do, so I would have had to say no in that moment."

She felt the color drain from her face. That was not the answer she was hoping for, and she tried to stand. She couldn't sit here and wait for him to say anything more.

"Wait. I said in the moment."

She could hear the pleading in his voice. She hesitated and relaxed in the chair, but she didn't ask another question.

He pointed to the potato. "I know you might think I'm crazy or completely at a loss for words, and the whole potato thing worked so much better in my head than in reality. But that measly little potato is a symbol of how deep my feelings are for you. I want to share everything with you—my hopes and dreams, my life. Our life."

"Then why did you just say you wouldn't have stayed if I asked?"

"I needed to take the test for me, to see if I had recovered and if physically, I was the same person before the accident, and I found the answer to that in Chicago. I'm not the same person." He let go of one of her hands and tapped his forehead and then the center of his chest. "Something changed when I met you. I discovered something about myself. I wanted to have someone in my life who encouraged and supported me, who challenged me when I struggled, and you've become that person for me, and I hope I've given you some of the same things too. But before I could ask you to share any part of my life, I had to make sure I knew what it was going to be."

Her heart flipped. "Are you going back to fighting wildfires and jumping out of planes?" She cupped his cheek in the palm of her hand. "If you are, I can handle it. I care about you too much to try and change who you are in here." She placed a hand on the center of his chest. She could feel his heart thudding.

"That's the best thing you could have said."

Now she was going to have to back up those words with actions, but it was true. Since Tric, she had time to think and knew the best relationships allowed each partner to be their best self. If Tric wanted to save the forests, then she would be by his side figuratively.

He gave her a lopsided grin. "Kel, I said I passed the test and training was going to be starting soon, but I never said I was going to attend the training and take my spot on the squad. I could, but I don't want to. If it's okay with you, I'd like to move to Last Chance Beach and have a *real chance* with you."

That was the sweetest thing she had ever heard. "I can't ask you to give up what you love."

"Silly woman, you didn't. I made the choice and it was

the only decision I could make, given that I would be doing a disservice to the people I work with, knowing that my mind was here with you and not totally focused on the job." He searched her face. "What do you say? Are you okay with me moving down here and we can start dating like an average couple?"

"You're walking away from a career that you love for me?" She hated that her voice rose by the time she got to the end of that sentence. "You can't do that. Someday you might resent me for it, and that would be the end of whatever we had."

"I'm not walking away. I'm going toward what I really want—you." His eyes twinkled. "And I learned something else while I was in Chicago. I had a couple of beers with my Uncle John who is friends with your Uncle Kevin, and it seems those two put their heads together and cooked up the whole thing about me renting Shamrock Cottage so that we could meet. They decided to play matchmaker specifically to get us together."

"What are you talking about? You said you rented the cottage through the agency." And then it dawned on her. "But that was after the two of them set it up and neglected to tell either of us that funny business was at play." She laughed while she shook her head. "Wait until I talk to my uncle again."

"Don't be too mad at him. After all, their instincts were right and we go together like sand and sunshine."

"Even so, they didn't need to meddle." She could feel a small smile hover on her lips. It had worked, so she really couldn't be mad at anyone. So much for her thinking that the magic of LCB led Tric to her. "Do you want to move back into the cottage with me or find a place of your own?"

"Call me a little old-fashioned, but I think a place of my own is in order to give us both some space to get settled in our new whatever you want to call it, and then who knows what will happen next."

"What about work? You can't stay in a motel for long. That is expensive."

"Listen to you, always practical. It's just one of the things I love about you."

Her breath caught.

"I do love you, Kelly." From his pants pocket, he pulled a small, slim box wrapped in shamrock paper and tied with a thin green ribbon. "I brought you a little something."

"You shouldn't have." She brought her eyes up to meet his. "But I do love presents."

He handed it to her and said, "Open it."

She carefully eased the ribbon off and slit the wrapping paper. She wanted to savor this gift from him. Her shamrock tiara slid forward and she pushed it back before taking the lid off the white cardboard box. She knew it was some kind of jewelry, but what?

"I'm sitting here, wondering what you got me, when all I have to do is look inside and I'll have my answer. Anticipation is half the fun." She leaned in closer to him and gazed into his eyes and touched his cheek. "I can't believe you're really here."

He kissed her again. "Anticipation is half the fun and although I couldn't agree with you more, I'd really like you to take the top off. I'm so excited for you to see it."

He grinned while she did as he asked. She folded back the green tissue paper and with a laugh, said, "You really got into this whole festive vibe, right down to the wrapping paper."

"Nothing you don't deserve."

Tucked inside was a Celtic knot necklace in the shape of a shamrock, and in the center of the knot was an emerald. The chain was strands of fine gold threads and she held it up. "Tric, this is stunning, but way too much."

"You deserve to have something very special. When you wear it, you'll think of me."

"I don't need a necklace to be reminded of you."

She flung her arms around his neck and pulled him close, kissing him. "This is the most thoughtful thing anyone has ever given me. Thank you so much." She handed him the necklace. "Will you put it on for me?" She lifted her hair as he fastened it behind her neck. She touched the knot and murmured, "The symbol of faith, hope, and love."

"You gave me all of those things long before tonight." He nuzzled her neck. "And this is just the beginning."

A thrill raced through her. "I like how that sounds." She caught Judy looking at them, her eyebrow cocked. "I'd like to go show it off."

"You go ahead; I'll be right there." He pulled her into his arms and gave her a warm kiss filled with promise of what was to come.

Tric watched as Kelly floated across the room to her friends. The women were taking turns admiring the necklace while he waited in line for his turn to place their drink order. She gave him a sweet look over her shoulder before turning back to the ladies. Surprising her had been the perfect choice. He'd always remember the look on her face when their eyes met and how she felt in his arms. When he had hit the ground in September, broken and bruised, he would never have guessed that it would turn out to be the beginning of his chance for happiness.

He took their pints of beer and crossed the room to the woman he loved. After he handed her a glass, he said for her ears alone, "I haven't forgotten about the breakfast you made me."

Her eyes danced with merriment. "There's more fun where that came from too."

Before their lips met, he said, "I can't wait."

EPILOGUE

The Following Summer

*K*elly's family was coming to the Ryan family cottage at Lake Geneva for July Fourth weekend. Her cottage at Last Chance Beach was rented for the summer season and she and Tric were looking for their own cottage on the lake. They planned to be waterside for the year, half lakeside and half in Last Chance Beach, a perfect combination. Boston would have to wait another year since this was the first time the two families were meeting and it was the perfect time for her to surprise Tric. She double-checked the inside pocket on her handbag to make sure the box was still there. Not that she thought it would disappear, but she was nervous.

"Kelly?" Tric's voice drifted up the stairwell. "Your family has arrived."

"Coming." She zipped the pocket and hurried downstairs. Let the party begin.

· · ·

*T*ric stood to one side as Kelly's aunt held her close and his parents hugged everyone. It was a perfect summer day at the cottage, with the sun bright in the deep-blue sky. The fish were biting, and he was sure the two families would blend perfectly like corned beef and cabbage.

He couldn't help but notice how much Kelly looked like her family. He hoped someday they'd have a daughter who looked just like her. "Tric, this is Uncle Kevin and Aunt Joan." She held out her hand.

Her eyes were bright and if he hadn't known better, he'd suspect she had been working on her practical jokes, but they had agreed on no pranks for this weekend. He had to be on his best behavior too. But he hadn't agreed to no surprises, and when they were sitting around the fire tonight, he was going to ask Kelly a very important question. He patted his shorts pocket to reassure himself the box was still there.

*E*veryone had pitched in to clean up from dinner and now chairs circled the fieldstone firepit. The heat from the blaze kept the mosquitoes and the dampness from the evening chill away. Kelly was sitting close to him in a wide chair and his arm was draped casually around her shoulders.

She said, "Does anyone need anything? I'm going to run in and get a sweater."

Uncle Kevin piped up and gave an exaggerated wink. "Tric, you're not doing your job keeping your girlfriend warm."

He wrapped both his arms around her and pulled her close. "Working on it, Kevin."

She wriggled out of his embrace and pecked his lips. "I'll be right back."

"I'll be waiting."

He watched as she hurried across the lawn, then through the screen door. It closed with a soft *thud*. The light in their bedroom came on briefly and then off. He tapped the box still in his shorts. It was almost time.

*K*elly struggled to contain her excitement. Her hand quivered as she popped open the top on the box, but she didn't have a single doubt he'd say yes.

As she approached the fire, she rehearsed, for the final time, what she was going to do and say. Standing in front of Tric, she held out her hand. He took it and she pulled him to his feet, turning him so everyone could see his face.

"Honey, what's going on?"

She placed a finger over his lips. "For once, let me start."

He grinned.

"Once upon a time, there was an Irish lass who moved to Last Chance Beach to run away from love. Then our uncles decided to play matchmaker from a distance and rent you Shamrock Cottage. It was decided that there was an Irish lad for this lass after all."

She pulled a small box from behind her back and knelt down on one knee. She popped it open and inside was a Claddagh ring, the symbol of love from Ireland.

"Tric, I'm not a traditional kind of girl and you are certainly not a traditional kind of guy because up until a year ago, you were crazy enough to jump from an airplane and fight wildfires. So, Patrick Ryan, I would like to ask you if you'll do me the honor of marrying me."

Tric dropped to one knee in front of her and he held out a small white velvet box. When he popped the top, sitting inside was an emerald and diamond ring. "My love, my anam cara, my soulmate. There isn't anyone else I'd want to walk through life with. How about on the count of three, we answer each other?"

She blinked back happy tears and he brushed his thumb over her cheek.

"One."

She said, "Two."

In unison, they said, "Yes."

Slipping the rings on each other's fingers, the family was forgotten as they sealed their future with a kiss.

It was only after a few minutes that Uncle Kevin said, "Last Chance Beach and Shamrock Cottage can change your life."

Kelly and Tric laughed. "Forever."

The End

Click here for the next Last Chance Beach book:
Everything's Coming Up Daisy
By
Nancy Fraser

Kristen Matthews is a single mother of a precocious four-year-old named Daisy. They've recently returned to Last Chance Beach to live with Kristen's elderly aunt. However, with the move comes the possibility of revealing a secret Kristen's held onto since before Daisy's birth.

Ellis Tait is the uptight head of Tait Holdings—an astute business man who can juggle boards of directors, investors, and his competition. Yet, dealing with a four-year-old boggles his mind.

A modern twist on the classic *Sabrina*. Can this single-mom avoid her ex's family and hide the fact that her daughter is heiress to the family fortune? Or, will the island magic of Last Chance Beach unite an overworked mom and curmudgeon of a family patriarch in time for a happily-ever-after?

Universal purchase link: https://
books2read.com/LCBDaisy

MORE BOOKS BY LUCINDA RACE:

Preorder:

Apple Blossoms in Montana: An Orchard Bride Novella

Last Chance Beach

Shamrocks are a Girl's Best Friend March 2022

The Crescent Lake Winery Series 2021

Blends

Breathe

Crush

Blush

Vintage

Bouquet May 2022

A Dickens Holiday Romance

Holiday Heart Wishes

Holly Berries and Hockey Pucks

It's Just Coffee Series 2020

The Matchmaker and The Marine

UNTITLED

The MacLellan Sisters Trilogy
Old and New
Borrowed
Blue

The Loudon Series
The Loudon Series Box Set
Between Here and Heaven
Lost and Found
The Journey Home
The Last First Kiss
Ready to Soar
Love in the Looking Glass
Magic in the Rain

ABOUT THE AUTHOR

Award winning and best-selling author Lucinda Race is a lifelong fan of romantic fiction. As a girl, she spent hours reading and dreaming of one day becoming a writer. As her life twisted and turned, she found herself writing nonfiction articles, but longed to turn to her true passion: novels. After developing the storyline for the Loudon Series, it was time to start living her dream.

Lucinda lives with her husband Rick and two little pups, Jasper and Griffin, in the rolling hills of Western Massachusetts. Her writing is contemporary, fresh, and engaging.

Visit her at:

www.facebook.com/lucindaraceauthor

Twitter @lucindarace

Instagram @lucindaraceauthor

www.lucindarace.com

Lucinda@lucindarace.com

Made in the USA
Las Vegas, NV
18 April 2022